"Congratulations, Ms. Marshall—you have just hit the jackpot. You are the lucky winner of twins."

Nikki stared at Seth, certain she couldn't be hearing correctly. "What do you mean I won them?" she croaked finally.

Seth shrugged. "I could have said you *lost* the lottery, but I thought it would make you feel better if I put a positive spin on it. What it comes down to is, you get to keep the twins a while longer."

Nikki's head was spinning. "Oh, no."

"You're the one who volunteered for this responsibility," Seth pointed out.

"I said I'd take care of the babies for three days. Count them—Friday, Saturday, Sunday!"

"Or until Laura gets home."

And Laura didn't expect to be hit by a virus, any more than I would expect to get struck by lightning... But what was she going to do about it?

Couldn't Seth help...?

Leigh Michaels has always been a writer, composing dreadful poetry when she was just four years old and dictating it to her long-suffering older sister. She started writing romance in her teens and burned six full manuscripts before submitting her work to a publisher. Now, with more than 75 novels to her credit, she also teaches romance writing seminars at universities, writers' conferences and on the Internet.

Leigh loves to hear from readers. You may contact her at:

PO Box 935, Ottumwa, Iowa 52501, U.S.A. or visit her Web site at www.leighmichaels.com

ASSIGNMENT: TWINS

Leigh Michaels

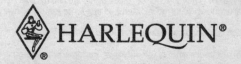

HARLEQUIN®

TORONTO • NEW YORK • LONDON
AMSTERDAM • PARIS • SYDNEY • HAMBURG
STOCKHOLM • ATHENS • TOKYO • MILAN • MADRID
PRAGUE • WARSAW • BUDAPEST • AUCKLAND

ISBN 0-373-03836-4

ASSIGNMENT: TWINS

First North American Publication 2005.

CHAPTER ONE

NIKKI plunged her hands into the hot, soapy water for the last time and pulled the plug out of the drain. "There, that's the last of the dishes." She picked up a baby bottle which had tipped over and set it upside down to drain on one of the towels which lined the small counter.

From the dining nook just outside the galley kitchen, Laura called, "Washing three days' worth of my dirty dishes wins you the friendship service medal, you know."

Nikki dried her hands, rolled down the sleeves of her silky blouse, and buttoned her cuffs. "Is that all I did?" She kept her voice light. "From the size of the pile, I expected it had taken a week to build up."

"For the average family of four, perhaps. But when you have two kids this size, dirty stuff collects in a hurry."

Nikki paused in the doorway. Laura was sitting with her back to the kitchen, facing a pair of high chairs. In each chair was a dark-haired child, not quite a year old, each armed with a small, soft-tipped spoon and a plastic bowl. The thick, gooey, grayish, slimy-looking substance which had once been in the bowls was now spread liberally over the high-chair trays as well as the two cherubic faces, and a few lumps had landed on the plastic mat which covered the floor.

All things considered, Nikki thought, *I got the best end of the deal by doing the dishes.*

Laura's babies were adorable, no question about it. But fond as Nikki was of Zack and Anna, she didn't regret that her life had taken a different channel from Laura's. At least, not very often.

"What is that stuff they're eating, really?" Nikki asked.

"Rice cereal mixed with mashed pears."

Nikki wrinkled her nose. "It looks like library paste that's been left out to mildew."

"Shh. They're very sensitive to other people's reactions to food. I mashed up some squash for them to try the other night. Stephen took one look at it and made gagging noises—and the twins spit out every bite after that."

"You're certain it was because of their dad? I mean, honestly, Laura—squash? They're only eleven months old. Not liking squash seems to be part of the deal."

"It's an excellent source of Vitamin A," Laura said firmly.

"I'm sure it is." Nikki nodded toward the twins. Zack had cereal in his left eyebrow. Anna's chin was covered with half-dried paste. "Are they actually getting any of that stuff inside where it counts?"

"Well, Anna's better at it than Zack is," Laura admitted. "But Zack's more determined to do it himself, so I have to sneak in an extra bite when he's not paying attention." She dipped a spoon into one of the bowls and inserted it into the boy twin's mouth while he was inspecting a lump of cereal that had stuck to his smallest finger. He swallowed absent-mindedly and opened his mouth again.

"Want me to help?"

Laura smiled. "You don't really mean that. If you got cereal all over that suit right before you go meet an important client, I'd feel awful. You've already done enough for one day, anyway, clearing up my dishes. Having a broken dishwasher and two babies does make life a little difficult."

Nikki pulled up a chair. "I know finances have been a

bit tight lately for you and Stephen," she said gently. "But it will have to be fixed before you can list the house for sale."

Laura nodded. "Seth's going to tear it apart when he has time and see if he can get the parts so he and Stephen can get it running again."

"When he has time? I see." Nikki was proud of herself; her voice sounded absolutely neutral. "How's The Lone Repairer doing these days?"

Laura shot her a suspicious look. "Since when do you want to chat about Seth?"

"I was just making conversation. But if you don't want to talk about your husband's brother—"

"I thought you might have run into him recently. He's working on a house up in the Rockhurst neighborhood, one of those huge mansions near the art museum. It's a big job."

"And that—plus all the blond fashion-model lookalikes who require his attention—is why your dishwasher is still broken."

"Well, I do wish he'd date someone whose IQ is larger than her dress size," Laura said. "But to be perfectly fair, my dishwasher isn't Seth's responsibility. He has his own place to keep up."

"I suppose when it's your full-time job to fix things, it's not much fun to do it on your day off, too."

"It would be sort of like asking you to go on a tour of homes for fun, after you've shown houses all week long."

"I happen to love home tours, but I see what you mean. It's too bad Stephen wasn't the brother who inherited the handyman genes."

Laura sighed. "The poor guy tries. He put up a towel rack in the bathroom last week."

"Without Seth supervising? I'm amazed."

"Of course, it fell off three days later and tore a chunk out of the tile wall."

Nikki winced.

"At the rate we're going, we'll never get this house in shape to sell. Of course, if we can put it off till the kids go to college, we won't need to buy a bigger house at all. The next eighteen years will be something of a challenge, in a two-bedroom house with no playroom and a kitchen the size of a postage stamp, but—"

"This is a darling house, Laura."

"That's the real-estate person inside you talking."

"It's a cute little cottage with an efficient floor plan. Perfect starter home for a young couple."

"Until they unexpectedly have twins." Laura spooned cereal into Anna's mouth. "Stephen wanted me to ask you something. A favor."

Surprise tingled through Nikki's veins. It wasn't that she and Stephen never talked, but it was generally Laura who issued invitations and arranged plans for the couple, while her husband was the quiet, always-agreeable one. For Stephen to specifically ask Nikki for a favor…

Laura went on hastily, "I already told him it wouldn't work, but you know how guys can be—once they get an idea, there's no blasting it out of their heads. I had to promise him I'd ask, so I'm asking. But honestly, Nikki, I've already told him you can't, so there's no problem."

"Well, that seems to settle it," Nikki said cheerfully. "But maybe you should tell me what the favor actually is, honey? I mean, in case Stephen should bring it up, it would help if I have a general idea."

"Oh." Laura grinned. "I guess you're right. There's this thing he has to attend next weekend. His boss was scheduled to go, but at the last minute he's had a conflict, and so they're sending Stephen instead. And he wants me to go with him.''

"So you need a baby-sitter? What's the big deal? Of course I'll—''

"It's not just an evening, Nikki. It's a conference. Sort of a continuing education seminar that goes on all weekend.''

"Well, that does make a difference,'' Nikki admitted. "He actually wants you to hang around waiting for him while he's taking classes? I hope you can at least go shopping.''

"It's on a cruise ship in the Caribbean.'' Laura sounded wistful. "But I've already told him I can't go.''

Nikki stared at her. "Of course you can. Are you nuts, Laura? How many times do you get a free second honeymoon?''

"Well, it wouldn't exactly be free. We'd have to buy my plane ticket. And I called a couple of babysitting agencies— Do you know what they charge for round-the-clock care for two babies for a weekend?'' She shivered.

"I can imagine. So Stephen wanted you to ask me to look after the twins so you can go.''

Laura nodded. She looked unhappy. "I know how busy you are—''

"You said it's next weekend?''

"A long weekend, actually. Friday morning to late Sunday night.''

"I don't have any open houses scheduled over the weekend, so—''

"What about dates? Are you still seeing Richard?''

"Once in a while. It's no big deal.'' She saw Laura start to open her mouth, and hurried on before the questions could start. "All I'd have to do is clear my calendar for Friday.''

"Nikki, please don't feel obligated to do this. Even Stephen admitted that it would be a lot to take on for anyone who isn't used to twins. He'll understand that you can't do it. He's just disappointed right now."

"What about you?" Nikki asked gently. "Are you disappointed?"

Laura didn't look at her. "Of course I am. We could never afford a cruise on our own. But I'd probably be seasick anyway, so—"

"Not on a ship that size. You're going, so start packing." Nikki picked up her suit jacket from the back of a chair. As she was putting it on, she looked past Laura to the twins and hesitated. Both of Zack's eyebrows were now daubed with cereal, and Anna had a bit on her nose.

Three days. Alone. With twins…

"Wave bye-bye to Aunt Nikki," Laura prompted the twins.

Zack was too absorbed in turning his bowl upside down and watching it drip to pay attention. Anna gurgled, grinned, and waved her spoon in the air. A blob of cereal flew off and splatted against the lapel of Nikki's jacket.

Laura sighed and held out a damp washcloth. "Sorry about that. I won't hold you to the offer, Nikki."

Nikki scraped the blob off with her thumbnail and rubbed the dark blue fabric with the corner of the washcloth. "I'll just move my name tag up to cover the spot," she said. "Come on, Laura. You do this all the time. Surely I can handle it for three days."

Nikki had taken care of the twins before, of course—for an evening now and then to let Stephen and Laura go out for a sandwich and some adult talk, and once in a while for an afternoon so Laura could get her hair cut or see a doctor. This would be no different, she told herself. Only longer.

Much longer, she realized on Saturday afternoon as she took the twins out of their stroller after a walk. She was exhausted because Zack had awakened at two in the morning with a nightmare and it had taken an hour to get him settled again. She'd already run through every activity she could think of and built so many block towers to be knocked down that she was qualified for a job putting up a skyscraper. And she hadn't even looked at the briefcase full of paperwork that she'd brought with her.

And they were not quite halfway through the weekend. She had just as many hours stretching in front of her as had already passed.

What she'd failed to take into account was that the twins at eleven months were far more active and inquisitive than when they had been infants. They were no longer charmed by the slow revolution of a mobile above a crib. Peekaboo and pat-a-cake were no longer exciting. Not only had they had been actively annoyed at being strapped into the double stroller, but they'd made it clear they were highly insulted when Nikki refused to let them kiss all the neighborhood dogs.

By the time she untangled Anna's safety harness and extracted her from the stroller, Zack had already crawled into the narrow space between the couch and the recliner in pursuit of his ball, and got himself stuck.

Zack started howling at his predicament, and Anna began howling in sympathy. Nikki was just drawing a breath and thinking about joining them when she heard the back door open and a deep voice call, "Anybody home?"

She gritted her teeth. Seth Baxter. The Lone Repairman had finally found time to look at Laura's broken-down dishwasher.

Why right now? she wanted to shout. Why not last week, when Laura had been at home? Or if he absolutely had to come this weekend, why couldn't he have showed up that morning, during the fifteen-minute span when Zack and Anna had been contentedly playing with two empty boxes and a stack of plastic yogurt cups? Or last night after they'd been bathed and tucked into their cribs?

Of course, by the twins' bedtime she'd been practically a zombie herself, with pureed peaches and baby shampoo down the front of her sweatshirt...

Not that Seth Baxter would have cared what she looked like, anyway.

In the last two years, every time she'd ever come face to face with the man, he had acted as if he found her mildly interesting—worth one long appraising survey, but nothing more. She'd come to expect that no matter what she was doing or how she was dressed, Seth would scan her with that same slightly ironic gleam in his eyes, looking her over just long enough to make her want to scream—and then, as if the sight of her bored him to tears, he would turn his attention to something else. Nikki would rather have him ignore her completely, but she supposed the chances of that happening were nil.

Of course, all things considered, she didn't exactly blame him for inspecting her as if she were a curious breed straight out of the zoo, because that was pretty much the way she'd acted the first time they'd spent any significant time together—though his own actions hadn't exactly won any etiquette prizes.

She sighed and reminded herself to be grateful that she didn't run into him more often. Once every few months was bad enough.

"In the living room, Seth." She stooped to extract Zack from his predicament.

Seth came around the corner from the kitchen. "Nikki? What are you doing here?"

She snagged the back straps of Zack's overalls and tugged him out from under the edge of the couch. "Didn't anybody tell you about the cruise?"

"Yeah, Steve said something. I forgot it was this weekend." He leaned against the stubby wall which separated the living room from the dining nook, arms folded across his chest. "I wondered what they were going to do with the house apes. Zack, buddy, you've got to remember how to get yourself into reverse."

Nikki finished wiping Zack's tears and took a good look at Seth. It had been several months since she'd seen him—across a baptismal font, where he'd been holding Zack while she cradled Anna—but he matched the picture in her mind almost exactly. His dark-brown hair was sun-streaked and longer than it had been at the babies' christening, and he was wearing jeans and a polo shirt instead of a suit. But he was every bit as tall and lean as she remembered, his eyes were just as stunningly green, and his shoulders pushed the limits of the knit shirt. And the look...yes, there it was. Half-bemused, half-fascinated, and totally wary— the same expression that always made her want to scream.

Anna stopped crying, dropped to her hands and knees, and scrambled across the carpet toward Seth. He picked her up almost absently, still looking at Nikki. "How's it going?"

She was darned if she'd admit that a few minutes ago she'd been ready to howl along with the twins. "Great. We're doing fine."

"Uh-huh. How many times has Laura called?"

"From the ship? Just once, when they first got on board."

"That's amazing."

"She said she'd call back, but I heard Stephen in the background reminding her this was supposed to be a vacation. Anyway, she doesn't need to check in—she left a full list of instructions on the refrigerator door, right next to her appointment calendar.''

''Her list actually fit on the refrigerator? I'd have expected a whole volume—alphabetized and cross-indexed.''

Nikki smiled. ''Maybe she just didn't have time to write it all down. But it doesn't take an instruction manual to know that these two need a nap right now. I was just ready to put them to bed, so don't let me keep you from working on the dishwasher.'' She stepped closer to him, close enough to feel his warmth, and held out her free arm to take Anna.

The baby had nestled into Seth's shoulder, and she didn't seem inclined to move. Nikki stroked the baby's back. As her fingertips neared Seth's forearm, braced under Anna's bottom, Nikki felt tingles run along every nerve.

Don't be ridiculous, she told herself. *You've touched him before.*

At least... Well, she must have touched him somewhere along the way, she told herself, even if right at the moment she couldn't remember a specific occasion. They must have shaken hands when they were introduced, for one thing— though when she stopped to think about it, she couldn't remember actually meeting Seth. He must have just been part of the crowd, at some party back in the dark ages when Laura was dating Stephen and Nikki herself had been engaged to Thorpe. Perhaps it had been about the same time the four of them had started to make plans for a double wedding...

The dark ages, indeed.

Seth held the baby out so she could get a grip on Anna's waist. Nikki's hand brushed his arm, and she jerked back a little before she got hold of herself and very deliberately let her arm rest against his while he transferred the baby's weight.

He didn't say anything and neither did she. And it was utterly ridiculous for her to feel breathless over such a little thing. But—maybe she *hadn't* ever touched him before, because she'd have remembered that kind of smoldering heat.

Nonsense, she told herself briskly.

As if they were afraid of missing something exciting, the babies did their best to fight off sleep. Ultimately they succumbed, however, and Nikki tucked them into their side-by-side cribs and tiptoed out of the room.

The house was quiet except for the catchy rhythm of a jazz tune coming from the radio in the kitchen. The front panels of the dishwasher were propped against a cabinet door, and Seth was lying on his back on the floor, peering into the dark cavity underneath the machine.

Nikki stopped in the doorway. "Have you found the problem?"

"Not yet. The drain's not clogged, and the floats are working."

"Is that good news?"

"Nope. I've eliminated the simple stuff."

Which means he'll be around for a while longer. Just leave him to his work and go get your briefcase, Nikki. But she didn't move. "I'm going to make myself a cup of coffee. Want one?"

"Sure." He slid further under the dishwasher. "How are you, Nikki? It's been a while."

"Since we ran into each other, you mean?" She shrugged. "Three or four months, I guess."

"Three. It was at the christening, and you were scandalized that Laura had asked a heathen like me to be the babies' godfather."

Nikki didn't bother to argue the point. Instead she stepped across him and started putting water into the coffeepot. "How's Inga? Or was it Elsa you brought that day? I get your girlfriends all mixed up."

Seth smiled, but he didn't answer. Nikki wondered if that meant he'd forgotten the woman's name, too. Quite likely, she thought. All of Seth's girlfriends looked, sounded, and acted alike.

"How about you?" he asked. "Are you still seeing the stockbroker you brought to the christening?"

"He was a commodities trader," Nikki corrected. "The stockbroker was before that. And no—not for a while now. There's a banker I'm seeing at the moment."

"What happened to the commodities trader? He was practically glued to your side that day."

Nikki had to think about it for a moment before she remembered. "I realized that if I wanted to get a play-by-play of the day's markets, I could watch the financial channel—and turn it off when I got tired of listening."

He prodded at something deep under the machine. "What the… I hate working on antiques. I swear the motor's rusted into this thing. Being second-best never did appeal to you, did it, Nikki?"

She stopped spooning coffee into the filter and turned to stare at him. "Oh, now The Lone Repairer has expanded into psychology?"

He reached into the cavity with a pair of pliers, and she heard a metallic snap. "Still touchy about the wedding, I see."

Touchy. That was one way to put it, she supposed. "It's been two years, Seth. I've put it behind me and gone on with my life. So can you just forget it?"

He shook his head. "Of course not. That was one of the

great dramatic scenes of the age. I'll never forget watching you tell Thorpe where to get off.''

She plugged the coffeepot in and pushed the button to turn it on. "Next time I break an engagement," she said dryly, ''I'll be sure to invite you.''

"Don't bother. Nothing could ever top that one. Thorpe's already at the church, wearing his tux, boutonniere pinned in place, fussing with his hair and trying to cover up the signs of a really bad hangover, and you come storming into the ushers' room wearing half a wedding dress and shrieking at him like a banshee. The costuming alone would have been worth the price of a ticket.''

"I was *not* shrieking. I was making a point.''

"Not that you didn't have reason to shriek," Seth added. "Though I still think you went a little over the top when you started yelling at me. Just because I happened to be there to hear it all—''

''You could have let me know you were there, instead of hiding behind a pillar and listening to every word I said.''

"And interrupted your train of thought while you were on a roll?" He shook his head. "You were just lucky all the rest of the ushers had stepped out for a breath of fresh air so I was the only witness." He sat up and reached inside the machine, grunting as he tried to lift out the motor unit. "I admire you for doing that, you know.''

Nikki was startled. "For what? Calling off my wedding because the groom spent the night before the ceremony carousing with a bunch of call girls?''

"I think they'd probably prefer to be called exotic dancers.''

Nikki shrugged. "Same thing, as it turned out.''

"Anyway, that's not the reason. I admire you for going out in front of the crowd and facing the whispers because it was Laura's wedding day too, and you didn't want to spoil it for her.''

Why there should be a lump in her throat was beyond Nikki's understanding. She bit her lip. ''Thanks.''

''Anytime.'' The motor twisted, and Nikki heard a crack from somewhere deep inside the dishwasher. ''I didn't like the sound of that,'' Seth muttered. ''In fact, I think I may have found the problem. Or maybe I just created a new one. That's not my cell phone ringing, so it must be yours.''

Nikki hadn't even heard the buzz. That in itself was an indication of how badly the man got to her, she told herself as she retrieved the phone from her briefcase. ''This is Nikki Marshall.''

''Thank heaven. I thought you'd never answer.'' The voice was soft, feminine, and dripping panic.

Nikki recognized it—Jen was the youngest and least experienced member of the sales staff at the realty office. Why she was apparently on duty alone was beyond Nikki's comprehension. ''What's wrong, Jen?''

''The MacIntyres are here to make a counteroffer on the house they want to buy, and I don't know what to do. Can you come in right away?''

With two babies asleep in the next room? It had been difficult enough to take them for a simple walk through the neighborhood. Hauling them out of bed and across town to meet with a pair of clients would be torture. Unless Seth would agree to keep an eye on them…

She looked over her shoulder and saw him putting the panels in place on the front of the dishwasher. So much for that great idea.

''Out of the question, Jen.'' She ignored the woman's protest. ''Their file is in my bottom desk drawer. The client number is on the tab of the folder. Pull it up on the computer, find the offer they made last week, put in the new price, print out the form, and have them both sign it." She glanced at her watch. "Then call the delivery service— have a courier bring the papers here, and I'll check them over. Got it?"

Jen repeated the instructions and the address. "Okay," she said doubtfully. "If you're sure you can't come in."

"I'm sure," Nikki said, and snapped the phone shut. When she came back into the kitchen, Seth was putting the last screw into place. "Is it all fixed?"

"Far from it. I have about fifteen pieces to replace—if the home-supply store has them."

"Then why put it all back together now? You'll just have to take it apart later. I don't mind if it's in pieces—it's not like I'm getting ready for a dinner party tonight."

"Because I don't want the twins to rearrange all the pretty wires."

"Oh. Good point. You'll be back later, then?"

"Tomorrow sometime. I have an engagement tonight."

"With Elsa?" She kept her voice light. "Or Inga?"

"Neither. Why?"

That figured. By now, Nikki thought, there could have been half a dozen more tall, slim blondes in and out of his life. "Seth, you don't know the meaning of the word engagement."

"People who live in glass houses shouldn't throw stones, darling.... How many guys have you dated since Thorpe, anyway?"

"A few," she said coolly. "Why?"

"Anybody who's lasted more than a month?"

"I don't think so." She kept her voice deliberately light. "But then by your standards, a month is an eternity, so you don't need to worry about me being fickle. I'll see you tomorrow, if you don't want that coffee after all."

He shook his head. "I'll take a rain check. You know,

you look as if you could use a nap yourself, instead of caffeine.''

"I've got some work to do. I have a closing on Monday, and a new client coming into town—so I need to refresh my memory of the listings before I decide what to show him.''

"Him? I thought it was normally the woman who chooses the family home.''

"Usually it's the wife who does most of the looking,'' Nikki agreed. "But this guy's single. Actually, I think he's divorced. He's an upper-level executive with the auto-assembly plant.''

"Now that sounds promising,'' Seth said. "If you're really lucky, maybe he'll be like the commodities broker—and you can find out every step it takes to build a car.''

Nikki didn't know whether she was getting used to the routine, or the twins were accepting her, or they were all just too tired to make a fuss, but everything went a little more smoothly on Sunday.

The babies had already had their nap and were in their high chairs toying with their dinner when Seth arrived. He let himself in with a cheerful hello, set a large paper bag of parts on the kitchen counter, and gave the coffeepot a speculative shake.

"If you're hoping to have that cup of coffee you missed yesterday, you're too late,'' Nikki said. "I kept it hot for you till just a couple of hours ago, though.''

He made a face and started to take the bottom panel off the dishwasher again. "The truth is, you forgot to turn the pot off.''

Nikki put another spoonful of peas and carrots in front of Zack. With his index fingertip, he rolled a pea across the tray. Then he tried to roll a carrot chunk, and settled for smashing it into mush instead.

"How's it going today?" Seth asked.

"We're doing great, aren't we, kids?"

Anna gurgled. Zack noticed remnants of carrot on his fingertip and tried to shake them off.

Seth slid under the dishwasher. "How long till Laura and Steve get home?"

"Six hours," Nikki answered automatically. Too late, she tried to bite back the words.

Seth was grinning. "I'm surprised you don't have it figured out down to the minute. So you want to tell me how you're really doing?"

Nikki sighed. "I missed the courier yesterday because I was in the middle of a diaper change when he rang the doorbell. I yelled, but he couldn't hear me and I couldn't get there in time, so I have a counteroffer hanging in limbo because the papers are locked up in a delivery van till Monday."

"That's rotten luck."

"And this morning Zack was standing up in his crib when I went in—and the way his face crumpled when he realized that it was me again and not his mother almost broke my heart."

"Better you than a baby-sitter he doesn't know at all."

Nikki twisted around to look at him. "Don't you have any sympathy for the poor kid?"

"Of course I do. I'm just realistic about it instead of sentimental. It's good for them to get used to different people."

"Well, good luck convincing them." She added a few chunks of chicken to Anna's tray and handed the baby her cup of milk. "And while you're at it, try persuading Laura. Though she still hasn't called back." Nikki frowned. "Now that I think about it, it's a little strange that I haven't heard from her.''

''There hasn't been a word?''

Nikki shook her head. ''Aren't phone calls from a cruise ship pretty pricy? Maybe Stephen put his foot down.''

''He could try, but I don't think that would stop her any more than it would keep a mother bear from charging to defend her cubs. Are you in the mood for a bet?''

''Tell me what it is first.''

''Whether Laura calls the minute they land at the airport, or she rushes straight home to her darlings.''

''She'll call,'' Nikki said promptly.

''I don't think so. If she calls, she'll be five minutes later getting here.''

''It won't hold her up a bit, because she'll send Stephen after the car while she's on the phone. That's not a bet, Seth, it's a certainty—so the only question left is how much money you want to give me. Anna, smashed peas are not a good conditioner for your hair. Come on, sweetheart, let's go wash it out.'' She lifted Anna from her high chair. ''Do you mind if I leave Zack here for a minute, Seth? It's much easier to wash them one at a time.''

Seth waved a hand instead of answering.

When she came back, he'd turned the radio on and taken the baby out of his high chair. Zack had pulled himself up beside a dining room chair and was hanging on tight, swaying his bottom in an approximate rhythm with the music. Seth was on the floor, both hands out of sight underneath the dishwasher.

''Hold that bag down here for a minute so I can sort through it, would you, Nikki?''

She knelt, holding the bag out of the babies' reach. ''How are you doing?''

''So far I've managed to break another valve and increase Zack's vocabulary by at least two words that Laura doesn't want him to know.''

The music stopped and a newscast began, but Zack danced on, too fascinated by his own movement to notice. Anna watched him as if she was studying each step. Seth sorted through pieces. And Nikki, half-listening to the newscast over the rattle of metal parts and the babbling of two babies, caught a few words that sent chills up her spine.

''Cruise ship... Caribbean...virus...quarantine...''

She scrambled to her feet and made a dash for the living room.

''Hey,'' Seth called, ''where are you going with my bag of parts?''

Nikki didn't bother to answer. She dropped the bag in the nearest chair and dived for the television remote control.

The story was on the second news channel she checked. A mysterious virus had struck a cruise ship in the Caribbean, and public health officials were taking no chances. The ship and the two thousand people on board would be quarantined off the Florida coast until the bug was identified and the passengers were confirmed not to be contagious.

Nikki didn't have to hear the name of the ship; the sinking feeling in the pit of her stomach told her it was the one Laura and Stephen were on. ''Oh, no,'' she whispered. ''All those poor people, shut up on a ship together with stomach cramps and headaches and fevers—''

Seth stood in the doorway, listening intently. ''At least it doesn't seem as though the symptoms are life-threatening. Just miserable.''

''Somehow I don't think it would be a lot of comfort to know you're not going to die,'' Nikki mused, ''if you feel bad enough to want to. What a way to spend a vacation!''

"I wonder if Steve's boss will charge this up against his sick leave." Seth's voice was flippant, but there was a shadow in his eyes and a furrow between his brows.

"No wonder she hasn't called. There must be two thousand people waiting in line to use a phone, if they can even get out of bed long enough to dial."

"So we both lost the bet," Seth added, "because she won't be calling from the airport, and she won't be coming straight home, either. At least not tonight." He looked down at Nikki and raised one eyebrow. "Congratulations, Ms. Marshall—you have just hit the jackpot. You are the lucky winner of twins."

CHAPTER TWO

NIKKI stared at him, certain she couldn't be hearing correctly. "What do you mean I won them?" she croaked finally.

Seth shrugged. "I could have said you *lost* the lottery, but I thought it would make you feel better if I put a positive spin on it. What it comes down to is, you get to keep the twins a while longer."

Nikki's head was spinning. "Oh, no."

"You're the one who volunteered for this responsibility," Seth pointed out.

"I said I'd take care of the babies for three days. Count 'em—Friday, Saturday, Sunday. I'm—"

"Or until till Laura gets home."

And Laura didn't expect to be hit by a virus, any more than I would expect to get struck by lightning... But what was she going to do about it? "I wasn't counting on this." Her voice felt feeble. "They could be delayed for a couple of days."

"At least." Seth was looking at the television set.

Nikki followed his gaze. Someone from public health was showing off a chart of infection rates. The angle of the line tracing the increasing number of infected people aboard the ship looked like a rocket's path to the heavens. If her sales figures were to climb at that rate, Nikki thought, she'd be thrilled.

She said, trying to sound cheerful, "The good news is that at this rate the virus will have gotten to everybody on

25

the ship by about tomorrow. Once that happens, things can only get better, right?''

"That's what you call the good news?''

Nikki had to admit it didn't sound very encouraging. "Look, I'm not trying to make light of the situation. I'm as worried about Laura and Stephen as you are. But it looks as if they've got the entire public health organization working on it...'' Her words sounded hollow. That sort of no-holds-barred action wasn't directed at every garden-variety virus. This stuff was different.

Poor Laura had been afraid that she might get seasick on the cruise. *Now there's irony for you,* Nikki thought. Compared to the bug that was running wild on the ship, it sounded as if seasickness would be positively pleasant.

"No point in worrying. There's nothing we can do about Laura and Steve right now.'' Seth picked up the bag of parts and went back to the kitchen.

Nikki trailed him hopefully.

Zack had flopped down on the kitchen floor and was chewing on the handle of a screwdriver. Seth took it away from him and put it back in the toolbox atop the counter. The baby howled, and absently Nikki picked him up, handed him a plastic measuring cup from the cabinet and watched in disbelief as Seth snapped the toolbox closed.

"You're not leaving.'' It was half-question, half-plea. "Seth, I can't stay here till that ship's out of quarantine. I was supposed to go home tonight. I have a life, and I've already put it on hold for three days to do this.''

"What are you planning to do with the twins, then?''

Nikki opened her mouth to answer, and shut it again. What on earth *was* she going to do with the twins? Much as she hated to face the fact, Seth was right—she had assumed the responsibility, and now it was up to her to make sure the babies were safe and taken care of, until their mother could take over once more. If she couldn't actually look after them herself, then she'd need to find someone who could. She looked speculatively at Seth.

"The way I see it," Seth said, "you can look in the want ads under baby-sitters—"

"Hire a stranger? Laura wouldn't like that."

He didn't seem to have heard her. "Or you can call child protective services and report that the babies are being neglected, and have them put in foster care. Or you can drop them off on a stranger's doorstep, ring the bell, and run."

"Don't be ridiculous."

Seth shrugged. "That's about all the options I can think of."

"There's one more. I can hand them over to you. You're their godfather."

"Being a godparent has nothing to do with baby-sitting. It's purely a spiritual duty."

"Don't go getting sanctimonious on me now, Seth."

"I wouldn't dream of trying. You're the one who said it. As I recall, you told Laura on the twins' christening day that I was a bad choice for the position because I wouldn't recognize a spiritual experience if it bit me in the—"

"Seth Baxter, do you ever do *anything* when you're in church besides eavesdrop?"

"So you admit telling her that."

"I may have," Nikki admitted. "I don't actually recall. But that's beside the point."

"In any case, you're their godmother, so the same argument applies to you."

"All right then, we'll leave godparenting out of it altogether. You're their uncle. With their parents out of the country—"

"Don't forget *indisposed*," Seth added.

"That makes you their closest kin at the moment. I'm

only a friend of the family, with no legal standing at all. So the bottom line is that you're the one who has to make the decisions.''

Seth's eyebrows raised slightly. ''If it's my choice, then I choose to let you keep them. You've been doing a fine job so far.''

Nikki couldn't decide whether to scream or kick the nearest piece of furniture. ''I have a house sale closing tomorrow, and I can't even change the time because too many people are involved. I can't find a sitter by tomorrow morning because I haven't the faintest idea where to start looking. Seth, I'm begging. You have to help me out here.''

''Why me? You signed up for this duty. I didn't.''

''Because I can't take a set of year-old twins to a mortgage closing, that's why!''

''Well, I can't just hang them from my tool belt while I rebuild Mrs. Cooper's closets, either.''

Nikki bit her lip. ''I don't suppose you can. But surely you can put Mrs. Cooper's closets on hold for a day or two. At least till we find out what's going on on that ship.''

''Obviously you've never met Mrs. Cooper, or you wouldn't say that.'' He lowered himself to the floor and began to put the panels on the dishwasher once more.

As soon as he finishes, he'll leave. You have to do something, Nikki—and fast.

She put Zack down on the floor. ''How about that cup of coffee you were wanting earlier?''

''I expected better from you in the bribery department than that, Nikki.''

''All right,'' she conceded. ''I won't waste your time by making coffee.''

''The truth is, there are so many dishes in the sink you couldn't get to the faucet for water anyway.''

Nikki ignored him. ''Let's talk about this like adults. I

can't miss that closing. If you'll just keep the twins to-morrow morning—''

Seth was shaking his head.

"You won't even do that much? Just till noon." Nikki knew she sounded desperate. She didn't care.

"I can't. I've got a supplier delivering a load of materials at eight o'clock in the morning."

Nikki chewed her lip. "Eight? My closing isn't till half past nine. Maybe we can work this out after all. Surely that gives you enough time."

"Depends on how fast the crew unloads. It's a big or-der."

"Well, the closing is downtown. If I get the babies up in the morning while you go sign the receipt for your sup-plies, then I can swoop by and drop them off with you in Rockhurst—it's almost on my way—and go straight to the closing. You can bring them back here and—''

His eyebrows raised. "How do you know I'm working in Rockhurst?"

"Laura, of course." Nikki surrendered the last of her pride. "Seth, if you'll just bail me out for a couple of hours in the morning, I swear I'll come straight back after the closing."

"What about your new client? The fancy executive at the auto plant?"

She'd forgotten. For a moment there, she'd actually for-gotten a client, something which had never happened be-fore. *So it's not just an old wives' tale. Spending countless hours with babies really can turn your brain to mush.*

"I wonder whether he likes kids," Seth mused.

Nikki gritted her teeth.

"If he's divorced, maybe he has children of his own. He might even enjoy having the twins around. It's such a cozy little domestic image—you, him, the babies, looking at houses…''

Nikki had no trouble at all creating that picture in her mind. She sighed. ''I guess someone else will have to show him around tomorrow.''

''Hey, kids,'' Seth announced. ''She's giving up the tycoon for you. Bet you're tickled to hear that.''

Anna clapped her hands as if in delight. More likely, Nikki thought, the baby was pleased that she'd managed to pile all her plastic blocks into an unsteady tower. Now she was eyeing her brother's supply.

''Nobody else in the office could possibly be less prepared than I am,'' Nikki said almost to herself. ''I haven't even glanced at the multiple listings all weekend. All right, that covers tomorrow.'' She rushed on before he could argue the point. ''Now about tonight—''

''What about it?'' Seth sounded wary.

''I don't have any real clothes here, just jeans and stuff. I'm going to have to go home and get something to wear to the closing.''

''Do it in the morning.''

''It's impossible to get all the way out to my place and back downtown before half past nine. Not if I've got the twins, because they move like molasses in the mornings.''

''Then go shopping on your way.''

''You can't be serious. Try on clothes with two babies in tow? Besides, the malls don't open that early. And in any case, you can't just go and buy a copy of that blue jacket we have to wear—the real-estate company has them specially tailored.''

''Okay, okay, you made your point. Let's go.''

For a moment she was too thrilled at the hint of cooperation to take in what he'd said. Then it hit her. ''What do you mean, *let's go?* It will take me an hour. Ninety

minutes, tops. All you have to do while I'm gone is dunk
the kids in the tub, put their pajamas on, and tuck them
in.''

"That's all." It was obviously not a question.

"Hey, I've been doing it all weekend. I've gotten pretty
good at it, too." Nikki couldn't resist taking a jab. "You'll
probably still be wrestling with diapers when I get back.''

"I have a better idea. We'll all have an outing."

"You would actually drag two kids halfway across the
city at this hour just so you don't have to give them a bath?
Maybe it's just as well if you keep dating lame-brained
blondes, Seth. If you actually ever break down and marry
one, maybe she'll be dim enough not to notice that you're
ducking all the work."

"I'm not ducking anything. When we get back, we can
both pitch in for bath and pajamas, and we'll get it done
in half the time."

Nikki doubted it, but at least he sounded willing to try.
That made her even more suspicious of what he was really
up to. She stared at him, eyes narrowed, and finally all the
pieces clicked together in her mind. "You don't trust me
to come back at all, do you?''

"Would you trust me, if you were in my shoes? If I put
on my jacket right now and said I'd see you later—''

"Probably not," Nikki admitted.

"Then we understand each other quite well—and we're
square to start with.''

She said carefully, "You mean you'll actually help? All
that protest earlier about not wanting to be involved—''

"Earlier, you weren't asking for help. You were trying
to dump the whole mess on me.''

He was probably right, she admitted. Relief surged
through her.

"I'll pitch in, Nikki," he warned, "but don't get the idea

that you're off the hook. Come on, let's go get you some clothes.''

She went to get the twins' jackets from the stroller, which was still sitting just inside the front door. As she wrestled Zack's arms into the sleeves, the television bulletin caught her eye once more. This time the jumpy, grainy picture on the screen showed a helicopter hovering over the deck of a ship, lowering bundles of supplies. Everybody within range of the camera was wearing a surgical mask. A few were fully garbed in protective gowns and gear.

For a disease that wasn't supposed to be severe, Nikki thought, it certainly looked scary.

Seth came into the living room, with Anna already bundled in his arms. ''Are the kids' safety seats in your car?''

Nikki shook her head. ''I wasn't planning to go anywhere, so I didn't bother to put them in. Seth—what if they're not all right? Laura and Stephen, I mean. What if it's worse than the health department's saying? They don't take this sort of precaution for just any little bug.''

''Don't even think about it. Worrying won't help Laura and Steve, but it will sure upset the babies. In the meantime…'' He shrugged. ''You're the religious one. Pray that somebody figures out how to stop that virus in its tracks.''

Nikki had underestimated how long the trip would take. It was closer to two hours before Seth's SUV was back in the driveway. Anna was asleep in her seat, Zack was yawning, and Nikki felt like falling into bed herself.

Seth carried Nikki's suitcase and Zack, while Nikki wrestled a limp Anna out of her seat.

''I don't care how grubby they are,'' Nikki said. ''I don't even care how many of Laura's rules I've violated tonight. Let's just put them to bed in their clothes, and I'll give them a bath tomorrow.''

As soon as the twins were tucked in, she unpacked her suitcase, hoping that in her haste she'd managed to grab at least a few pieces of clothing that coordinated. Trying to suppress a yawn, she went back to the living room. Tired or not, she still had to look over the paperwork for tomorrow morning's closing.

Though she wasn't surprised to be doing her review at the last minute, she hadn't anticipated these circumstances. By now, Laura and Steve should be driving from the airport into the city. Any minute, they should be pulling up beside the house, unloading bags and souvenirs, chattering happily about the flight and the cruise, exclaiming how much the kids seemed to have grown in just a few days...

Don't let yourself start, Nikki.

The house was quiet. She looked around in surprise. Had Seth gone, without even a word? He'd followed her out of the babies' room, but where had he gone then?

He probably slipped out before I could think of any other favors to ask, she told herself dryly. Or perhaps someone was waiting for him. He hadn't mentioned another date, but that didn't mean he didn't have one.

She opened her briefcase and swore when the blinking blue light on her cell phone caught her eye. The light meant she had voice mail waiting for her—probably from the courier service trying once more to deliver the paperwork on the MacIntyres' counteroffer. That was yet another thing she'd have to deal with—or hand off to someone else—tomorrow morning.

She was truly off balance, she told herself, to have gone away and left her phone behind—and not even noticed that it wasn't in her pocket. *It figures,* she thought. The damned thing had rung only once all weekend, until she'd walked off without it—but now she probably had messages stacked to the ceiling.

She punched in the code to retrieve her voice mail. There was only one message after all. That was a small blessing.

Behind her, Seth said, "Give me your keys so I can move the safety seats into your car."

That was sweet of him, thinking ahead to make the morning easier for her. Nikki dug in the side pocket of the briefcase for her key chain, and froze as the message started to play. "It's Laura," she said and held the phone at an angle so Seth could listen too.

The connection wasn't the best, and there was so much background noise that it sounded as if Laura was calling from a New Years' Eve party. "Nikki, where are you? You always answer your phone—oh, no, I hope that doesn't mean something's wrong with one of the babies. I only have a minute—there are people waiting, so I can't talk long. We're fine, we don't have this—stuff, this virus, whatever it is. But they're holding us prisoner even though we're perfectly healthy—oh, all right, Stephen, I know my minute's up. Nikki, I'll try again when I can get back to a phone, but I don't know when that will be—you wouldn't believe the lines. I'm so sorry to do this to you. Kiss the babies for me and tell them Mommy wants to come home."

The message clicked off and there was silence.

Nikki tried to blink back tears. "Oh, damn, I wish I'd been here. I could have told her I'll take care of the babies—"

"She knows." Seth's voice was little more than a whisper.

Only when she felt the warmth of his breath against her cheek did Nikki realize how close his face was to hers. It had seemed so natural to share the phone, to tip it so he could listen, too. So he could share right away in any news, rather than her having to relay it. To be close enough to lean on him, in case the news was bad.

But now that they were practically cheek to cheek… She was almost breathless.

Don't be ridiculous, she told herself. *It isn't like there's anything romantic going on here.*

Oh, there were plenty of sparks between her and Seth Baxter, all right—there had been ever since that day at the church two years ago when she'd told Thorpe precisely why she wasn't going to marry him, and then she'd turned around to see Seth half hidden behind a pillar and drinking in every word as if it were hundred-year-old scotch.

But the sparks weren't the starry-eyed kind. Far from it, in fact. What the two of them created was the kind of grinding, gnashing spark which flared when metal scraped against rock—and heaven help anything that got between.

No, the reason she was feeling off-balance right now had nothing to do with Seth practically having an arm around her. She was just suffering from a sudden attack of sentimentality. Even if she'd expected that message to be from Laura, Nikki would never have anticipated how strongly affected she would be by simply hearing her friend's voice. It was no wonder if her first thought was to look for a supportive shoulder—it had absolutely nothing to do with who the closest shoulder happened to belong to.

She snapped the phone closed and took a step away from him. "Well, at least we know that Laura and Stephen are all right." She kept her voice cheerful. "That's good news. If they haven't gotten sick yet, they probably won't, and maybe they can leave the ship tomorrow." She dropped the phone back into her bag. "Oh, you wanted to shift the car seats."

Seth took her keys without a word.

Nikki pushed the high chairs aside and sat down at the dining room table with her papers. Though she didn't try to memorize the details of every transaction, she'd learned a long time ago that being able to explain each number, what it meant, and how it was calculated was almost certain to make the closing proceed more smoothly. When clients were signing documents that obligated them to thirty years of mortgage payments, it was no time for the real-estate person to appear uncertain or uninformed.

She flipped through the document and tried to page back to make a comparison, only to find the first sheet stuck to the table. How on earth, she wondered, had Zack and Anna managed to spread their lunchtime applesauce so far and so liberally without her noticing?

Seth came back inside as she was prying the page loose. "Thanks for moving the seats," Nikki said. "I'm always afraid I won't get them in right."

"I didn't move them. I'll take your car tonight, and we'll swap back in the morning in Rockhurst. Got a scrap of paper?"

"What? You're taking my car?"

Seth shrugged. "I looked at the back seat and decided it's easier to move my tools than the safety seats. See you at Mrs. Cooper's in the morning." He scrawled an address across her copy of the offer-to-buy, dropped his key on the table, and was gone before she could say anything more.

"Nice guy," Nikki muttered. "He just drives off in my car without even asking whether I mind."

But the longer she thought about it, the more relieved she was. Seth might be tempted to leave her stranded with two babies, but she was absolutely certain that he would never abandon her while she had possession of his SUV.

Seth caught himself checking his watch again. If Nikki was going to make it downtown on time, she'd better get her cute little tush—and his SUV—into gear. What was holding her up, anyway? Heavy traffic, perhaps. The Monday morn-

ing rush hour had been worse than usual. He just hoped
she hadn't stalled out on the freeway, or gotten into a
fender-bender. Maybe he should have turned himself into
a contortionist to get those seats into the back of her car
after all, instead of expecting her to drive his. She wasn't
used to a big vehicle—he knew that for a fact, because he'd
had to fold himself up to fit behind the wheel of her little
car.

He heard wood slam against concrete and wheeled
around to see one of the workers looking sheepishly down
at a scattered pile of lumber lying on the driveway. The
delivery crew foreman came around the back corner of the
truck and started to yell. "That's high-grade oak, you idiot!
Take it a few pieces at a time so you don't bang it up."
He called to Seth, "We'll get it all around back and then
we can inspect for damages, sir."

Seth nodded. He looked down the driveway again and
saw his SUV pulling cautiously off the street. *About time
she showed up.* Relieved, he walked down to meet her.

Nikki rolled the window down and leaned out. She was
already wearing her standard-issue dark-blue jacket, with
her engraved name badge clipped to the lapel. Her hair was
caught up at the back of her head in a knot that was held
together with what looked to Seth like chopsticks. The sunlight made it look more red than its usual medium brown,
and the breeze caught a strand and whipped it around her
face. She tucked it impatiently behind her ear.

"You're running late," Seth said. "I thought you might
have had trouble finding the place."

She looked indignant. "Not likely. For your information,
I know every address in Rockhurst. I've sold a good num-
ber of these houses. In fact, see the one across the street?
I've sold that one twice."

Seth couldn't resist. "Why? Weren't the first buyers

happy with it after all?'' He enjoyed watching her sputter for a few moments. ''You can park over there, out of the way of the delivery truck.'' He pointed at a narrow strip of concrete between the garage and a row of ornamental evergreens.

She didn't put the SUV into gear. Instead, she opened the door and slid out. ''If you want it out of the way, *you* park it. It was all I could do to drive this bulldozer. Putting it into a confined space is something I don't even want to think about. Where's my car?''

''On the street, just around the corner and out of the path of the truck.''

One of the babies wailed, and Nikki looked over her shoulder, biting her lip.

''The other one will start up pretty quick,'' Seth said. ''They probably think since they can't see you at the moment that you've disappeared forever. I'll get them out in a minute and they'll be fine.''

''They're a little cranky.'' She sounded a bit crochety herself, he thought, but the expression in her big hazel eyes was almost pleading. ''I finally had to wake them up or I'd never have made it. But there wasn't time to give them a bath, and they didn't want breakfast, so they'll no doubt be hungry in an hour or two.''

''Oh, that's just great.''

''Hey, I'm not the one who kept them up late last night,'' Nikki pointed out. ''But I've already had to face the music. It's your turn.'' She leaned into the SUV.

The tailored khaki trousers she was wearing molded themselves to a trim but nicely rounded bottom. Seth watched with appreciation until she turned around again.

She was holding not a baby, as he'd expected, but only her briefcase. ''See you in a couple of hours,'' she said. ''Have a good time.''

Both babies had started to cry in earnest. Seth smothered a sigh and opened the back door of the SUV. "Don't worry," he called after Nikki. "I'll make sure they have a nap so when you get back they'll be wide-awake and ready to entertain you!"

Nikki made a rude gesture over her shoulder and kept walking.

He grinned and unlatched Zack's safety harness.

"Sir." The foreman was standing right behind him, clipboard in hand. "If you can come around to the site now, we're ready for you to inspect the materials and sign the invoice."

Seth sighed and reached across Zack to lift Anna out. With a tearstained baby in each arm he followed the foreman around the corner of the house and past a trailer full of tools to the construction site.

At the back of the Mediterranean-style house a new wing, half as big as the original main floor, was taking shape. The poured concrete walls were ready for an eventual coat of stucco to match the rest of the house, half of the windows were in place, and the crates full of red tiles which had been part of this morning's load of supplies were now stacked neatly nearby, ready to go up on the roof.

Half a dozen men were already at work, but the instant Seth came around the corner of the house with a baby in each arm, everything stopped while the men gawked at him.

His crew chief grinned. "What's that, boss, a couple of new trainees? Couldn't get any with experience?"

Seth ignored him and made the rounds of the site, checking the counts and looking over the oak which the delivery men had piled inside the new rooms, safely away from rain. A couple of boards had splintered when they'd hit the driveway, and the foreman noted the damage. "Do you need the replacements right away, or can we just put them on next week's load?" he asked.

"Next week will be fine."

"I'll make sure they get on the truck then. All right, if you'll sign here...." The foreman looked uncertainly at him and the babies. "I mean..."

The twins probably didn't top twenty pounds each, but their combined weight, plus the fact that with both arms full he couldn't shift the burden to let one arm take a break, had left Seth's muscles aching. Moving stacks of two by fours—even tossing concrete blocks—was dead easy compared to walking around with a twenty-pound weight attached to each arm.

He thought about handing one of them to the foreman, but as if she'd read his mind, Anna grumbled and nestled closer. Well, the babies would just have to lump it for a minute, Seth decided. As long as he kept a close eye on them, they'd be as safe on the ground as anywhere.

He squatted down and set them on the lawn. Zack instantly grabbed a handful of the trampled grass and put it in his mouth. Anna yelped, clutched at Seth's jeans, and tried to pull herself to a standing position. He hoped his belt buckle wouldn't suddenly give way.

Seth signed the ticket, folded his copy, and stuck it in his shirt pocket, then bent to pick up Zack, who had green saliva trickling down his chin. "Come on, champ, spit it out," he ordered.

"And then we need you to move the SUV out of the driveway so we can get the truck out," the foreman added.

You can park over there, out of the way of the delivery truck, he'd told Nikki. But she had refused to move the SUV, and he'd forgotten to. He smothered a groan, picked up the babies, and hauled them back around to the front of the house.

The hell with it, he thought. It was only ten in the morning, but he might as well call it a day. He wasn't going to accomplish anything with a twin grafted to each arm, anyway. And since he'd have to buckle them back in again so he could move the SUV fifty feet, he might as well take them home where they could play in the grass without risking splinters and stray roofing nails.

Only after he got them both settled in the back seat and slid behind the wheel did he realize that his key wasn't in the ignition switch. In fact, it wasn't anywhere to be found.

Nikki's luck held. The traffic had lightened up in the few minutes while she was stopped in Rockhurst. And instead of having to drive five blocks past the bank and then get dizzy swooping around a parking ramp to find a spot to leave her car, she managed to filch the last parking place on the street directly in front of the building. It was a one-hour spot, however, and that helped to make her more brisk than usual at the closing, hurrying things along as much as she dared.

As soon as the last papers were signed, she stood up and started to briskly shake hands all around. "What's your hurry, Nikki?" the banker asked. "I thought you and I would have lunch at that new little bistro on Country Club Plaza."

"It's much too early for lunch."

"Of course it is," he said gently. "I'll pick you up at the office later."

"Oh—I'm sorry, Richard, but I can't. I have a long list for today." The excuse sounded—and felt—a bit feeble, but she didn't feel like explaining the twins, the cruise ship, and the virus in front of clients and bank staff. "I'll call you later in the week," she added, and gathered up her briefcase.

Richard Houston didn't look pleased, but he didn't argue.

The new homeowners had stopped on the sidewalk to wait for her, to thank her and invite her for dinner as soon as they got moved in. Nikki smiled vaguely and said she'd be in touch, and she practically ran to her car.

It had been locked while she was in the bank, of course, and the sunshine pouring through the glass had heated the leather of her seat till it was buttery soft and soothingly warm against her back, helping to relax the tension in her muscles.

The heat also seemed to have activated the scent of the leather—and something else, she noticed. Something clean-scented and musky and vaguely familiar. Seth's aftershave, she concluded. She wondered how long that aroma would linger.

At the office, she gave the finished paperwork on the closing to Jen to be filed, picked up her messages, and looked wearily at the courier package which had finally come full circle back to the office. She'd probably better deliver it in person rather than take a chance on another delay.

"Also, Bryan wants to see you," Jen added. "He's in his office."

No doubt her fellow salesperson was going to rib her about the MacIntyres' counteroffer, Nikki thought. Well, there was nothing she could do about it now except smile. Telling Bryan what had really happened to sidetrack the courier package would only amuse him more.

Bryan was on the phone, so she started to walk on past his cubicle. But he beckoned her in and waved her to a chair while he ended his call. "It's an important day for you, Nikki. I thought perhaps you'd like a hand to figure out your strategy for Neil Harrison."

The auto-plant tycoon. At least it wasn't about the

MacIntyres. Not that Nikki was any happier to be talking to Bryan about Neil Harrison, especially since she was going to have to admit that she couldn't stick around the office long enough today even to meet the man, much less show him houses.

"It's nice of you to offer to help," she said. "As a matter of fact—"

"Oh, I'm happy to give you my advice," Bryan went on. "It's all in finding the right strategy, Nikki. You know, of course, that men look at houses differently than women do. Women will look at anything and everything which vaguely resembles their needs. They'll make a full-time job of house-hunting, while men want to look at just one place and be done with it."

Ordinarily Nikki would have objected to the generalization, but today she didn't have any room to maneuver. Bryan might be a sexist jerk at times, but he was a good salesman—and he was in a position to bail her out of a jam. If she asked him for help directly, however, he'd never let her hear the end of it.

It's all in finding the right strategy, Nikki, she told herself. "You know, it's funny," she mused, "but I was just thinking about that very thing. The original call came to me because of the ordinary rotation, but I was wondering if Mr. Harrison wouldn't rather have a man show him around."

Bryan didn't react at all for a moment. Then he said, sounding wary, "That isn't like you, Nikki. Not grabbing a challenge—and the chance at a big commission."

Nikki tried to look innocent. "I just want to do what's best for the firm. You're right that this is a very important client, and I'd much rather have you make the sale—and get the commission—than for me to fall short and get nothing."

Bryan propped his elbows on the arms of his chair and clasped his hands together. "What's wrong with him, Nikki?" Suspicion dripped from his voice.

"Wrong? Nothing, as far as I know. I've never met the man. I just thought you could probably read his reactions better than I could. You know, man to man."

Bryan hesitated, then smiled slowly. "Well, that's certainly true. All right, I don't have anything better to do this afternoon. Which property were you going to show him first?"

"I hadn't decided yet," Nikki said truthfully. She wasn't about to volunteer that she hadn't even started to make a list, much less prioritize it. "And I wouldn't want to cloud your judgment, anyway. Let me know how it goes, all right?"

She dug into her briefcase for her car key, and pulled out two. Her own, and Seth's.

He was going to kill her. Worse, she didn't blame him.

It was just past noon when Nikki got back to the house. The SUV was in the driveway, and she breathed a sigh of relief—though she still almost tiptoed into the kitchen, wary of fallout.

Seth was washing dishes while the twins played on the floor at his feet, creating a mad symphony with pan lids for cymbals and wooden spoons for drumsticks. He looked up when she came in, but he didn't comment.

Relieved, she set her briefcase on the counter and picked up a towel. "I guess the fact that you're here means you must have a spare key."

"Now I do," Seth said dryly.

Nikki bit her lip. "I'm really sorry. It's force of habit to never leave a key in the ignition. Living in the city, driving in all kinds of neighborhoods…"

"Oh, think nothing of it. You could have automatically locked the doors with the twins still inside." He rinsed the last plastic bowl.

Nikki looked at the pile. Laura had been right—it didn't take long to create a mountain of china, glass and plastic. "Something tells me this is bad news for the dishwasher."

Seth nodded. "It's completely shot. I hoped I could substitute a new style of motor, but it's just too ancient to find one that will fit."

"Laura's not going to like that."

"It can't be helped. I'm going back to work, Nikki. The babies are all yours."

All yours. That sounded ominous. Was he planning to come back at all? He hadn't promised anything beyond this morning… "Look, Seth, I said I'm sorry about the key."

"I heard you. They've had lunch, by the way."

"I see that. I'm just surprised they'll eat spinach, if they won't touch squash."

Seth paused in mid-step. "Spinach?" He sounded as if he'd never heard of it before.

"Yeah." She gestured. "The green stains down the front of Zack's shirt. I'm not complaining, mind you, but you might try a bib next time." She wanted to ask, *Is there going to be a next time?*

"Sure. I'll keep that in mind."

She followed him to the door. "Is there anything you'd like for dinner?"

"Dinner?"

"I thought maybe… I guess not." She fumbled for a change of subject. "That's some closet you're building for Mrs. Cooper."

He raised an eyebrow. "You saw it?"

"Of course. What do you think? As soon as I realized I

had your key, I went straight back to Rockhurst to make sure you weren't stranded.''

He looked at her for a long moment. ''Anything's fine,'' he said quietly.

''What?''

''For dinner. I'll eat anything, as long as it isn't mashed or pureed. Or stuffed with spinach.''

Then he was gone, leaving her leaning against the counter, dishtowel in hand, smiling.

You're grinning like a fool, in fact, she told herself. What was so wonderful about it, anyway? She'd committed herself to cooking dinner for him. Not at all her sort of project.

But at least he was coming back.

CHAPTER THREE

Now she just had to decide what she was going to feed him.

Her cell phone buzzed, and Nikki fished it out of the pocket of her blue jacket and answered. For an instant, when she heard Jen's panic-stricken voice, she felt as though time had folded in on itself. But it couldn't still be Saturday afternoon, and she'd taken care of the counteroffer as soon as she'd found out that Seth wasn't stuck in Rockhurst after all...

"It's Mr. Hamilton," Jen said.

The auto-plant tycoon. "Oh, Jen, I'm sorry. I was in such a hurry to get out of the office this morning that I forgot to tell you that Bryan's taking over Mr. Hamilton for me."

"Bryan told me."

"Well, then..." *So why are you calling me?* "If you'll just send him back to see Bryan—"

"I tried," Jen wailed. "I told him you were sorry you couldn't meet with him and Bryan would be happy to help. He said he didn't want Bryan, that he'd talked to you and he didn't intend to start over with somebody else. I finally told him you'd gone home with a headache this afternoon, and he said..."

"Stop and take a breath before you suffocate, Jen. What did he say?"

"He said in that case he'd come back tomorrow at ten o'clock sharp and he certainly hoped your headache would be better. Bryan's furious, and the boss is starting to ask where you are—Nikki, you have to be here tomorrow. You just have to.''

And the fact was, Nikki thought morosely, that Jen hadn't even really told a lie—because Nikki could feel the headache coming on right now.

Nikki ran a practiced eye over the house. It was almost dusk, and she'd been working frantically for hours—but all her effort had started to pay off.

The living room was picked up for the first time since Laura had left, with only a few toys still strewn on a blanket where the twins lay. But neither of them seemed interested at the moment in blocks or rattles. Anna was sleepily chewing on the toe of her pajamas, while Zack seemed to be studying how the light fixture which dangled above him was put together.

The dining room table was ready. It had taken a while to scrub all the applesauce off it, and Laura's linen closet didn't seem to run to tablecloths. But Nikki had found a couple of nice place mats with matching cloth napkins, and she'd pressed a big pottery bowl into service as a wine cooler. All that was left to do there was to light the candles.

In the kitchen, the aroma of dinner rolls and twice-baked potatoes wafted from the oven, and a pair of steaks marinated, waiting to be put on the grill.

By the simple—and somewhat desperate—method of putting the twins in the tub with her, Nikki had even managed a bath, and she was wearing a coordinated slacks and sweater set.

Everything was ready when she heard the SUV in the driveway and then the click of the back door as Seth came in. Nikki struck a match to light the candles, looked up at him over the flare, and almost forgot to blow out the flame.

He'd stopped dead in the doorway between kitchen and

dining room to stare at her. Then, as if he couldn't bear to look at Nikki any longer, his gaze drifted over the burning candles, the neatly-set table, the wine bottle, and back to Nikki's face.

Understanding dawned. "Hey, don't look at me as if I've suddenly sprouted fangs," she protested. "Truly, I'm not treating this like some kind of a date."

She saw him swallow hard. "Of course you're not." His voice sounded a bit hoarse. "The candles, the wine... I'm sure you do all that every time you sit down for a sandwich."

Nikki was starting to feel annoyed. "All right, maybe I went a little overboard, but I just thought we could have a nice dinner. That's all."

"What are we celebrating?"

"Getting through the day," Nikki snapped. "Isn't that enough?"

"Well, I'm glad to have that cleared up. It would have put me right off my food if I thought you were trying to seduce me."

"In your dreams, Baxter."

"Or, possibly, my nightmares," he said sweetly. "So if this isn't some sort of weird date, what is it? A public relations campaign for domestic bliss?"

"You're joking, right? I have better things to do than try to illustrate to you the benefits of settling down. I'll leave that thankless chore to Laura."

He seemed to relax. "I'm sure if that's what you had in mind, Nikki, you'd be more subtle about it than Laura is. But even you have to admit that at a glance the picture looks pretty much like an ad for home sweet home."

He was right, as a matter of fact, Nikki realized. The twins—squeaky-clean, well-behaved, and looking like the front of a baby-food jar. The candlelit table for two. The

sensual aromas of sharp cheese, hot bread, and marinade...
No wonder he'd gone pale, wondering what she was up to.

"Sorry to shake you up," she said. "I'm so used to
adding a touch here and there to show a house off and
impress the prospective buyer that it just comes naturally
to do things like fold the napkins into fancy shapes. I'll get
out the paper ones if it'll make you feel better."

"To impress the prospective buyer," Seth mused. "And
what exactly am I supposed to be buying?"

Nikki gave up. "It's no wonder you've never gotten married, Seth—you start running even when nobody's chasing
you. The grill's already hot—just throw the steaks on,
would you? I'll tuck the babies in and be right back."

To her mild surprise, even the twins cooperated, going
down into their cribs without complaint for once. Maybe
they were all adjusting to the new order of things, she
thought. When Laura got home...*whenever* Laura got
home...she was going to see a big change in her babies.
The idea made Nikki feel sad.

Seth was opening the wine bottle when she came back.
"What's wrong, Nikki?"

"I was just wondering again when Laura and Stephen
might be home. Did you happen to hear any news about
the ship today?"

He shook his head.

"I tried to keep an eye on the television," Nikki said,
"but I didn't see anything at all. It's weird how something
can be a headline event one day, but it doesn't even matter
the next."

"You must have been pretty busy all day, too." He
handed her a glass. "How did you manage all this? You
can't have gone to the supermarket."

"No," Nikki said gently, "I couldn't—because, in your

hurry to get back to work, you forgot to take the car seats out of your SUV.''

He winced, but his voice was casual. ''Well, I guess between the key and the car seats, we're even. So if you couldn't go anywhere, how did you do all this?''

''Fortunately there are delivery services, and I raided Laura's cupboards for the rest.''

''Or maybe I should ask *why* you did all this.''

''Are we back to that again? I'm not trying to impress you with my domestic skills, Seth.''

''No, I mean why didn't you just put out a plate and a knife and tell me to fix myself a peanut butter sandwich?''

She should have anticipated that question, Nikki realized. If she was mad at him about the car seats, why had she gone to all the trouble? She shrugged. ''Well, I did invite you for dinner. And unlike you on the subject of your key, I just decided not to rub it in about the car seats.''

''I'm glad you told me that you aren't making a big deal out of it,'' Seth said. ''Otherwise I might not have noticed how nice you were being.''

''Glad to help you out.'' She glanced at the clock above the sink. ''If you like your steak rare, it's probably ready.''

''I'll give it another minute. Unless you prefer yours still cold in the center?''

She shook her head. ''Medium for me.'' She got the salads out of the refrigerator, where they'd been crisping, and set them on the table. ''We don't have much choice in salad dressings, I'm afraid. Oil and vinegar, or the bottled stuff that was in the refrigerator. I forgot to put any on the list—not that I know what you like best, anyway.''

''Oil and vinegar's fine.'' He got a plate from the cabinet and went out onto the deck, returning a couple of minutes later with two sizzling steaks. ''I'll turn the grill off now, unless you're going to need it for bananas flambé or something.''

Nikki's attention was on how to remove twice-baked potatoes from the oven without upsetting them and squeezing all the stuffing out. ''No, it's chocolate cheesecake for dessert,'' she said absently.

''You mean you even have dessert covered? Admit it, Nikki. You're buttering me up for something. Out with it.''

Nikki sighed. She'd hoped to put it off a little longer, until he was well-fed and relaxed—but it was obvious Seth was reaching his limits. ''Well, there *is* a little favor I need to ask.''

''That's a relief.''

''It is?''

''Yes. At least now I know I'm not going crazy.'' He held her chair and sat down across from her.

Nikki picked up her glass. ''To Laura and Stephen—may they come home soon. Actually, this wine isn't bad, for something the deliveryman recommended.''

''Let's get to the favor,'' Seth reminded.

Nikki shook out her napkin and picked up her fork. ''It's about tomorrow, Seth. I did my best to clear my calendar, but it turns out I have to go to work after all.''

''And you think I don't?''

''But you have a crew. They can keep right on building Mrs. Cooper's closets whether you're there to supervise or not.''

''Let's not even go into that. What's so important about tomorrow?''

She was reluctant to tell him, and surprised by her hesitation. What difference did it make? It was a reasonable question, after all. ''It's the tycoon.''

''I thought you were sending someone else to show him houses.''

"I tried. But he doesn't seem to want someone else."

He was looking doubtful.

Nikki started again. "It seems that he and Bryan didn't hit it off at all today, so he's coming back tomorrow to—"

"Bryan, huh? I wonder if he'd have been more adaptable if the substitute had been named Brenda instead. Never mind. How much of your day is the tycoon planning to take up?"

That sounds like a positive reaction, Nikki told herself hopefully. At least he hadn't turned her down flat.

The trouble was that Seth wasn't going to like the answer to his question. She supposed she could just blithely tell him it would only take an hour or two, and then hope like mad that Neil Hamilton would fall in love with the first place she showed him....

But that was no more likely than the idea that Seth might not notice when she turned up six hours late. No, it would be best to tell the truth and get it over with. "I have no idea, Seth. Probably the whole day. If I show him all the listings at the office, then I might only have to take him out to see three or four houses in person. But—"

"But each one will take an hour or two."

"By the time I drive him there, he looks around, and we drive to the next one—yes."

"So you want me to take charge of the twins all day. Nikki, I can't work with both arms full."

"Well, neither can I. *You* try opening an unfamiliar lock with a baby in each arm."

"Maybe your tycoon will be delighted at the opportunity to be a gentleman and open the doors for you."

"And maybe..." Nikki thought better of it and swallowed the rest of the sentence.

"How about taking their stroller? At least you wouldn't have to carry them."

"And take it in and out of the car at every house? Have you ever lifted that monster?"

"All right, bad idea. But at least once you're inside a house you can put them down and let them crawl—you don't have to carry them all the time."

"Oh, really? What if I put them down in some stranger's house and they pull over a vase and break it?"

"Better than breaking themselves. Do you have any idea how many dangerous spots there are on the job site?"

"So you take the stroller."

"And leave them in it all day?"

"Sure. They can nap, they can eat, they can observe—"

"They don't make hard hats that size."

"Oh, you're funny, Seth. Look, I'd be perfectly willing to pay a sitter. In fact, I tried to hire one—but I found out the hard way that the ones on Laura's list are all kids, so they're in school during the day." She sawed a bite off her steak. It wasn't that the meat was tough, because it wasn't—but Nikki felt like destroying something. "And I can't bear to just dump the babies off with someone they've never seen before." *And neither can you. At least, I hope you can't.*

"So we split," Seth said.

"What are you talking about?"

"We each take a twin. With one arm free, you can open doors and point to special features, and I can draw diagrams and sign checks. Neither of us will be in top form, but we'll both at least be functional."

Nikki was aghast. "Take a baby with me while I show houses?"

Seth shrugged. "It's either take a baby with you, or take both of them. Your choice."

There was a note of finality in his voice that made Nikki bite her tongue. Inadequate as the arrangement was, it was obviously the best deal she was going to get, and if she kept arguing things would only get worse. "I'll take one," she said.

"Smart woman." Seth dipped his fork into his twice-baked potato. "Hey, this isn't bad, Nikki. I had no idea you could cook so well. I'll be happy to help you out any-time—you can bribe me whenever you want."

They moved into the living room with their coffee and chocolate cheesecake, so they could watch the television for any further information about the cruise ship and the mysterious virus that plagued it. But the news channels rattled on about the latest celebrity wrongdoings instead, and finally—sick of listening—Nikki pulled her feet up under her, propped herself up with sofa pillows, leaned her head against the back of the couch, and said, "Tell me about Mrs. Cooper."

Seth turned the sound down to a faint whisper. "Mrs. Cooper? Why?"

"You told me you were rebuilding her closets. I thought you meant you were putting in new shelves or something."

"That's how the project started out—a fairly minor re-model. She wanted to turn the small bedroom next to hers into a walk-in closet and dressing room."

"And she ended up with a whole new wing instead? Was that your idea or hers? Because if it was yours, Seth, you're wasted in construction. You should be selling office build-ings."

Seth shook his head. "I just do what the customer wants."

"Even if it's totally impractical?"

"You don't get anywhere in this business by telling the customer what they *should* want. That just makes them go hire a different contractor."

"But you don't get anywhere by giving them something they won't be happy with, either." Nikki sighed. "You asked me about that house across the street from Mrs. Cooper's and why I'd sold it twice. You were right, you know."

"About the original buyers not being happy with it?"

She nodded. "It was the first big piece of property I ever sold, and I was so excited at putting the deal together that it didn't occur to me that this couple wasn't the Georgian mansion type. It's a great house, but completely impractical for them."

"How long did it take them to figure it out?"

"About six weeks."

"Ouch."

"They didn't blame me, but I always felt I should have asked a few more questions. Made sure they didn't just jump into something without thinking it through."

"So you think Mrs. Cooper's new wing is impractical."

Nikki was startled. "Did I say that? I didn't mean to. I was speaking generally. If someone wanted you to build them a house that was half-Oriental and half-Tudor, would you do it?"

"I might try to nudge them toward one style or the other," Seth admitted. "I do have a reputation to protect."

"And you'd also discourage them because in the long run, they wouldn't be happy with the contrast, and they'd never be able to sell it."

"Do you always think in terms of how hard something will be to sell?"

"Of course," Nikki said calmly. "A house is the biggest, most expensive single thing most people ever buy. It makes sense to consider what's going to happen when they don't want it anymore—whether that's next year or decades in the future. For instance, if instead of a ground-floor master suite, Mrs. Cooper was building an aviary so she could breed parrots and cockatoos—''

"Funny you should mention birds. If she had a hobby, maybe she wouldn't be watching like a hawk as every nail goes in. And she might even quit issuing change orders every twenty minutes."

Nikki giggled.

Seth stretched both arms out along the back of the couch. "So how do you know it's a master suite?"

"Well, you did say she started off wanting a new closet and a dressing room, so it seemed a reasonable assumption. Besides…'' She shot a sidelong look at him. "I walked through it today."

"You just strolled in and took a look around?"

"I was hunting for you," Nikki pointed out.

"Even though the SUV was gone."

"I didn't know it was gone. You might have pushed it around the back of the house out of sight."

He grinned. "Your excuse doesn't hold water, Nikki."

"All right," she admitted. "I wanted to see what you were doing. I thought from what Laura's told me that you were—'' She stopped, just a little too late, and bit her lip.

"A sort of odd-job handyman."

Nikki was relieved that he didn't sound as if her misinformed opinion bothered him any. And why should it? What did Seth Baxter care what she thought he was? "Well, yes. What do you call yourself, anyway?"

"General construction contractor."

"Well, that covers a multitude of sins. What exactly do you do?"

"My company builds houses, puts up additions like Emily Cooper's, converts garages to offices, remodels kitchens, turns warehouses into lofts. My ordinary crews handle most of the work, and if we get into something more specialized, we subcontract it."

"I had no idea," Nikki admitted.

"Well, we could probably while away the whole evening talking about all the things you don't know about me, and vice versa."

He was right, of course, Nikki thought. Just because they cared about some of the same people didn't make the two of them pals. They might have known each other for two years, but in fact they were barely even acquaintances.

And if they were to spend the evening playing twenty questions, they'd probably just confirm that they didn't have anything in common at all except for Laura and Stephen and the babies. So it was completely illogical to feel as if, somehow, she'd lost a friend.

"Talking about our differences would certainly be more fun than watching the news channel in mime... Look, there it is. The ship. And there's a number to call for information." Nikki sat up abruptly. Her foot slipped from under her, knocking the remote control off Seth's knee, and as they scrambled for it beneath the coffee table, they bumped heads. By the time they were upright again and he'd turned up the sound, the story was over and the phone number had disappeared.

Nikki groaned. "Did you catch any of that at all?"

"No. But surely they'll come back to it." He leaned back once more. "Why did you assume that we have nothing in common?"

"Hmm?"

"You seem to think if we compared our likes and dislikes that we'd find nothing but differences."

She redistributed her pillows and settled back against them. "And you think we'd be mirror images? All right, I'll play the game. What's your favorite music?"

"Jazz."

"Classical for me," Nikki said. "Food?"

"Steak. I've got you there, haven't I?"

"No, you don't. I chose the steak because it was in Laura's freezer, and I had pegged you as the meat-and-potatoes sort. I'm a seafood person, myself. Way to work off stress? And I don't mean the sort of exercise that involves a blond model."

Seth grinned. "In that case, playing racquetball."

Nikki made a face. "Too energetic for me. A nice long walk, followed by a bubble bath. So far, you're zero for three. Sure you want to keep going?"

"Only if I get to ask the questions."

"But then you can tailor your answers to fit, in order to prove your point."

"And you haven't been doing that? Come on, Nikki. When I started your car last night, there was a jazz CD in the player."

"That was jazz based on a classical theme, and—"

"Laura keeps mostly fish and chicken in her freezer, so you must have had to dig to find that steak. As for racquetball—" He shrugged. "Okay, I'll believe the walk and the bubble bath. I say it's two for three. Favorite hobby?"

"Needlepoint," Nikki said firmly.

His eyes widened. "But that's astounding. I learned to love needlepoint at my mother's knee, with the…uh… hooks and wheel and…"

She flung a pillow at him. "It would be a more convincing lie if you got your terminology straight, Seth."

He fielded the cushion and handed it back. "All right, does it count if I'm willing to learn? You can teach me."

"Not me. I mean—" She caught herself. "I mean—I don't take students."

Seth was laughing. ''What you mean is you were lying your head off.''

''I wouldn't know needlepoint if it bit me,'' Nikki admitted.

''Well, *that's* something we have in common.'' He sobered. ''You're exhausted, aren't you? Go to bed. I'll sit here a while longer, till they run the story again.''

Nikki yawned. ''Now who's sounding domestic?'' She felt herself turn candy-apple red. ''Oh, no, that's not what I—''

''—meant to say. I know. Go get some sleep. I'll check on the babies before I go.''

In the master bedroom, she swapped her slacks and sweater for sweat pants and a T-shirt, telling herself that her fashion choice had nothing to do with Seth still being in the house. It was just more practical to dress warmly. The extra pajamas she'd grabbed in her brief foray home were lightweight and frilly, and she'd practically frozen last night when Anna had awakened in the wee hours, needing a drink of water and a cuddle. This time, she'd be ready.

And if she needed to get up with the babies while Seth was still there...well, there was no sense in letting him suspect she was trying to be seductive, when in fact it was the last thing she wanted.

So if you haven't got seduction on the brain, a little voice whispered, why did the concept even cross your mind?

How long was he going to stay, anyway? Until the station ran the story again, he'd said. But was that likely to be a few minutes, or a few hours?

She lay down on the bed, remembering the way Seth had stretched out both arms along the back of the couch, his muscles flexing. The back of her neck tingled, as if he was still close enough to touch her. The sole of her foot still felt warm from brushing against his knee as she had pushed herself up. And the top of her head throbbed where she'd bumped into him—though it wasn't a painful sort of throb but an excited one. She felt as if the room was spinning.

With the last of her energy, she pulled the comforter up over her. How did Laura do this every day? And why, she wondered, hadn't Laura ever told her that Seth wasn't just some glorified maintenance man after all? Why hadn't she corrected Nikki's wrong impression?

Because it just wasn't important enough for her to bother with.

And it shouldn't matter now, either, Nikki told herself. In fact it *didn't* matter to her.

At least, not much.

She wondered if he was still sitting out there, waiting for the story. Perhaps she should just peek out and see whether he'd gone. And if he hadn't…

Nikki, you are losing it, she told herself firmly. She turned onto her side and pulled the comforter over her head.

Nikki woke with a sense of doom, feeling as if she'd missed something important—something along the lines of a college final or a job interview. She'd slept deeply, and if the twins had awakened in the night, she couldn't remember it. Maybe she was learning to sleepwalk.

Or maybe she just hadn't heard them. She frowned at the bedroom door and chewed her lip. The door was closed, though she remembered leaving it half open so she could hear the twins more easily. Or was she remembering a previous night?

With Seth still sitting out in the living room, would she really have left her door open? Surely not—and it was just as well, too. She could imagine the reaction if he'd happened to see a half-open bedroom door. He'd probably think that she was hoping he'd come in—and then he'd no doubt start giving her that half-bemused, half-fascinated look again. The look which had so annoyed her throughout the last two years.

The look, come to think of it, that she hadn't seen since he'd first shown up to work on the dishwasher on Saturday.

Don't get your hopes up, Nikki, she told herself. The look would no doubt be back as soon as the immediate crisis was past and he had the leisure to observe her once more.

She heard Zack and Anna chattering away, in the baby babble which she was only now starting to comprehend. But the sound wasn't coming from their bedroom.

How had they gotten out of their cribs? What on earth were they doing—and why did they sound so happy about it?

Nikki took the corner into the dining room with her bare feet screeching on the hardwood floor and stopped dead. The babies were in their high chairs. Zack banged his fists on the tray, Anna reached up to Nikki and uttered a non-sensical-sounding sentence, and Seth, standing in the kitchen, said, "How do we work this breakfast thing, kids?" He turned around to look at the twins as if he fully expected an answer, and focused on Nikki. "Hi, there."

"You're here early," Nikki said. She ran a hand over her hair. Not that it would do any good, she thought. She felt—and no doubt looked—as if she'd been on a binge the night before. But then, she realized, Seth looked a little rumpled himself.

"Not exactly."

She frowned. "You mean you just stayed?"

"Yeah. You'd only been gone ten minutes when the news story about the ship ran again, so I knocked on your door to tell you about it."

"I didn't hear you."

"That was obvious," he said dryly. "You were so far

gone I thought it would be safer for everybody if I stuck around. So I sacked out on the couch.''

"I don't know what to say." She moved past him and reached for the box of baby cereal.

Seth shrugged. "Just doing what needed to be done."

"Thank you," Nikki said slowly. She handed him a bowl. "Stir this up, will you?"

He grabbed a spoon, pulled a chair around, and sat down in front of the high chairs. By the time Nikki had finished mixing the second bowl of cereal, he was in a rhythm—a spoonful for each twin in turn.

"You're using the same spoon to feed them both?"

"It's efficient," Seth said. "Besides, twins who chew on toys together share every germ in the western world anyway, so what's the difference? They're not complaining."

"Just don't let Laura catch you at it." She handed each of the twins a spoon.

"Go get dressed," Seth said. "We can handle this end. And I'll have to stop at home and get some clothes before I can go to the job sites, so I'd like to get going as soon as possible."

"Okay. If you're sure." Odd that he'd said *get some clothes*, rather than just *change clothes*, Nikki thought. Unless... She said slowly, "What did the reports say about the ship?"

Seth didn't look up from the cereal-insertion assembly-line. "So far they've made no progress in figuring out what the virus is."

"Which means there's no end in sight."

"That's pretty much the size of it. Do you want to pick your twin for the day, or flip a coin to see which one you take?"

CHAPTER FOUR

NIKKI parked in her reserved spot just outside the real-estate office and eyed Anna in her rearview mirror. The baby's eyelids were heavy and her head was drooping to one side of the padded car seat. "You must have had Seth up before the crack of dawn," Nikki said, "since you're almost asleep again now. I bet he appreciated that."

No matter how he'd felt about it, of course, Nikki was certainly thankful he'd been there. How could she have slept so soundly that she hadn't even heard the twins wake up? It wasn't as if they were subtle about it—the moment their eyes popped open they started to babble, and the longer it took to get someone's attention the louder and higher-pitched the little voices became. She'd figured out after the second day that all Anna wanted first thing in the morning was a dry diaper. Zack, on the other hand, didn't give a rap about personal hygiene—he was simply afraid that something exciting might be going on outside his field of vision, so he was determined to get out where he could see it.

All of which meant that the pair of them were impossible to tune out. Yet Nikki had managed to disconnect her responsibility button completely last night. It frightened her a little to think what could have happened had Seth not been there.

Knuckles rapped on the car window beside her. Nikki jumped and turned to see Bryan standing on the pavement, briefcase in hand, obviously—like her—on his way in to work.

She opened the door. "Good morning."

"Is it? I hadn't noticed. Is your headache better?"

From the tone of his voice, it was apparent that Bryan didn't believe she'd ever had a headache at all. Nikki didn't blame him. She made a mental note to talk to Jen; if the young woman was going to start manufacturing excuses, they might as well be believable ones. "I feel great. Look, I'm sorry about Mr. Hamilton. I have no idea how he got this fixation on me. I've only talked to him once, and that was on the phone."

"Well, next time you ask me to take over one of your clients, make sure it's somebody who actually wants to buy a house."

"What does that mean? He's moving here from Detroit—of course he wants to buy a house."

"Then why didn't he want to talk to me?"

Maybe he didn't like your attitude? "Perhaps he just has really bad judgment, Bryan, waiting for me when he could have had your full attention."

"Or perhaps he's just a tourist."

A tourist—real-estate slang for someone whose hobby was looking at houses, soaking up the agent's time but not seriously interested in buying. Not likely, Nikki thought. But there was no sense in arguing with Bryan about it. "Would you give me a hand with my briefcase?"

"Why?" He sounded suspicious.

"Because I will have my hands full." She opened the back door and leaned in to unfasten Anna's safety harness.

The baby grumbled something that sounded like "Kick" and tucked her head into Nikki's neck.

Bryan looked horrified. "What's *that?*"

Nikki considered playing it almost straight— *"It's an immature specimen of female homo sapiens. I picked it up at the pet shop.''* But she knew that wasn't really what Bryan was asking. She sighed. "It's a long story."

"Well, if you think I'm babysitting while you gallivant around Kansas City with Neil Hamilton—"

"It never would have occurred to me to ask," Nikki said truthfully. *In fact, I wouldn't dream of leaving a child in your care.*

"Well, as long as we have that straight…" With a brief-case in each hand, he led the way to the door. Nikki balanced the baby on her hip, slung Anna's diaper bag over her shoulder, and followed. Bryan was standing beside the door, obviously waiting for her to open it. "I have my hands full," he quoted, sounding almost saintly.

Nikki bit her tongue to keep from pointing out the relative weight of their burdens and pulled the door open. *It's going to be a great day,* she told herself. But the words echoed hollowly in her head.

In the warehouse district not far from downtown, Seth noted the dark-blue car parked outside the two-story building which housed both his business office and his loft apartment, and swore. He had hoped he could get upstairs to shower and shave before his secretary got to work, but the lights were already on in the office. And there was zero chance that Nora wouldn't have noticed when she came in that the SUV wasn't in its usual overnight parking spot.

He could dodge her by going around to his private entrance at the side of the building, but he might as well face the music up-front. From her desk right inside the big window, she'd probably already spotted the fact that he was wearing yesterday's clothes and twenty-four hours worth of stubble, and she was no doubt already filling in the juicy details.

Too bad the truth—unlike Nora's imagination—was dry as dust.

He lifted Zack out of the back seat, clamping the wiry little body under one arm because the kid insisted on squirming loose if held upright. His muscles protested every move. Laura could use a new couch as well as a dishwasher, he mused—one that was long enough for a guy to actually stretch out on.

Of course, last night it wouldn't have made much difference. With the scent of Nikki's perfume and the warmth of her body heat lingering on the cushions, he'd have been uncomfortable even if the couch had been the size of a basketball court. So much for the idea that sending her off to sleep would clear his head. All he'd accomplished was to free himself to think, once he didn't have to be on guard to spar with her.

He grabbed the duffle bag which Nikki had packed with everything she insisted he would need all day, and swore under his breath. What had she put in there, anyway? Bricks?

He pushed open the plate-glass door of his office with his shoulder and backed through.

His secretary eyed him over her half-rimmed gold glasses. Then she lifted her pencil off the column of numbers she was adding, stuck it into the upswept gray hair above her right ear, and rubbed her chin thoughtfully.

Seth watched her for a moment, contemplating. It seemed to him that every woman past a certain age dreamed of being a grandmother—and if she didn't have her own family to spoil, she'd coo over whichever babies happened to come along. Surely this particular woman was no exception to the rule. And Zack couldn't be in safer hands than Nora's.

He decided it was worth a try. "Look what I brought you, Nora," he said cheerfully.

Her voice was dry. "I hope that means you have a box of Xavier chocolates tucked in the duffle bag."

"Nope. Something a lot sweeter than that." He set the bag down and juggled Zack into an upright position. "Hey, fella, say hi to Nora."

"That's what I was afraid you meant. Where'd the baby come from?"

"Nora, dear," Seth chided. "I never thought I'd have to explain the facts of life to you. He's not mine, I've just borrowed him for a while. I'd be willing to share."

"In other words, you're stuck with him and you're looking for a way out. This isn't in my job description, you know."

"You can write yourself a glowing recommendation for your personnel file."

"Or I could just give my notice and retire. Oh, all right, give him here—as long as you don't mind if the month's invoices go out late." She pushed her chair back and came toward them, arms outstretched.

"You're a love, Nora," Seth said. He started to hand the baby over.

But Zack had other ideas. He clung like an octopus, his sharp little fingernails digging ridges in Seth's neck. When Seth tried in self-defense to detach him, the baby planted his tiny shoes firmly on Seth's belt and pushed himself upright. Tears rolled down his cheeks.

Nora retreated, sitting down on the edge of her desk. "The young man seems to prefer you," she said pleasantly. "Goodness knows why, when you carry him around like a football."

Seth shot a disgusted look at her. "Hey, it's not our fault

that females just don't understand how men think, right, Zack?''

"I suppose there's no accounting for tastes," Nora mused.

Seth wasn't listening. "All right, buddy, we're in this together. Hey—ouch! Chill out, champ, or I'll put you in the duffle bag and zip it. You win, okay?"

Zack sniffed and buried his face in Seth's shoulder.

"And take your tongue out of your cheek, Nora." Seth started toward the stairs.

Nora held out a message slip. "Before you go, the foreman called from the Cooper site this morning."

Seth glanced at the page and groaned. "What in hell does she mean, she wants to move a window?"

"She said she couldn't live with that particular view," Nora said pleasantly.

"I hope he told her it was too late to change it."

"No. He thought that breaking the news was your job, as the boss."

"This was supposed to be a small project. Remodel her closets, she said. Put in a few shelves. At this rate we'll still be tied up there five years from now." He started for his office.

"Maybe she just likes having a bunch of well-muscled men running in and out," Nora mused.

"The same way you do?"

"Absolutely. Why do you think I keep coming to work despite you, anyway?"

Seth closed the office door behind him. He set Zack on the floor, ignoring the baby's vociferous protest, dropped into his chair, and punched in Mrs. Cooper's number. At first he'd decided there was no point in putting her on his speed dial because the job would be done in a matter of days. Of course, that had been six months ago. Now there was no point because her phone number was so deeply engraved on his brain that he'd probably still be able to recite it from his rocker on the porch of the retirement home.

A sultry voice answered with a trill.

"Mrs. Cooper," he said.

"Seth, how nice of you to call back yourself. But why must I keep asking you to call me Emily?"

Because the last thing I want to do is encourage you. "My foreman tells me there's some disagreement about a window."

"Well, yes. I walked in this morning to review the job, and it suddenly hit me—that window overlooks my neighbor's back yard. From the side of his pool, he could look straight into my new dressing room."

Hang a curtain over it. "Well, that's a big problem, Mrs. Cooper, because the wall around it is concrete."

"I know. That's what made it so obvious, you see."

"If you'd told me this a couple of weeks ago, when we were still putting up the blocks, we might have been able to do something. Now—"

"But I didn't recognize the problem till this morning," she said sweetly. "You can fix it, though—right? I'm certain you can fix anything."

"I'm afraid I—" Something was nagging at the back of Seth's mind, distracting him. Suddenly he realized what it was. Zack had gone quiet.

Too quiet.

He wheeled his chair around to see a small hump on the floor, draped in blueprints which had once been neatly rolled on the bottom shelf of the bookcase behind his desk. He made a grab for the roll and heard the sickening rip of paper—most of the drawings slid neatly off Zack's head, but what Seth hadn't been able to see was that one corner was clamped between the baby's brand-new pearly white front teeth. The kid had put a corner of the front elevation of the Andersons' not-yet-built house in his mouth and started chewing it up.

The baby gave him a wet grin and spit out the scraps. "Peek," he said clearly. "Boo."

Seth muttered an oath.

"Excuse me?" Mrs. Cooper's voice was frosty. "I am not accustomed to hearing that sort of language from some-one I'm doing business with."

"Sorry," Seth said. "It wasn't you, it was—"

Zack, deprived of his toy, crawled across the carpet and pulled himself up using Seth's knee as a brace. He reached up to the desktop for the blueprint he'd been chewing, and his flailing little hand hit the disconnect button on the phone. Suddenly Seth was talking to a dial tone.

"That does it, pal," Seth said. "Don't even ask, because there will be no summer internships around here for you." He punched in the number again and got only a busy signal. *Dammit.*

He swept up the baby and headed for the stairs. No time for a shower, but he could at least put on a fresh shirt and grab his razor so he could shave as he drove. "Nora, call Mrs. Cooper—and keep calling till you get through. Tell her I'm on my way over."

"You're headed the wrong direction," Nora pointed out.

She could say that again, Seth thought. He had a feeling that moving Emily Cooper's window would be only the beginning of the apology he'd have to make.

At precisely ten o'clock, Nikki closed the multiple-listings book, took a long drink of her now-cold coffee, and sur-veyed the list of addresses she'd assembled—houses which might possibly suit Neil Hamilton. There were twenty-three of them. It would take a week to show them all, so obviously she was going to have to cull the list somehow.

Voices approached her cubicle—Jen's high-pitched near-giggle, and a deeper, slightly nasal tone that Nikki remembered from talking to Neil Hamilton on the phone. That was a good sign, she thought. He'd obviously arrived on the dot.

Nikki stood up to greet him and felt her jaw drop as he came around the corner. He was a little older than she'd expected, and he didn't at all look like her idea of a hard-driving top executive but more like an old-time silent-movie star—thin, languid, graceful, world-weary, with smooth shiny black hair and dark, almost beady eyes. Though he wasn't actually wearing a cape, a sword, and a plumed hat, she had no trouble imagining how he'd look in them. She tried not to stare as she shook hands.

He didn't immediately let go of her hand. "Yes," he said. "You match your voice."

And you don't, Nikki thought a bit wildly. But perhaps that was why he was in the auto industry instead of motion pictures—because they'd have to get someone to dub all his lines…

"I'm very pleased to meet you," she said. "And sorry about getting a delayed start because of my absence yesterday. I have a fairly large number of possibilities, so I'd like to begin by getting a better idea of which features you consider absolutely necessary, so I can cut down the list. There's no sense in going to look at something if it obviously won't fit your needs."

"If you think I'd like it, Ms. Marshall—May I call you Nikki?—then I'll be happy to look it over. After all, I plan to live in this house for years. A few extra days to choose the correct one hardly seems unreasonable."

He was right, of course—though his timing could certainly have been a lot better. And she couldn't help but wonder if Bryan had been right when he called Neil Hamilton a tourist.

She took a firm grip on herself. Bryan, she thought, had probably been suffering a knee-jerk reaction to Neil's too-perfect looks. She wasn't going to make the same mistake herself.

"On the phone," she said firmly, "you mentioned needing a home office, of course, and a formal dining room for dinner parties, and at least three bedrooms."

He nodded.

"Is there a particular architectural style which you like? Or for that matter, one you hate?"

He shrugged. "Not that I can think of."

"Perhaps if you were to tell me about the kind of houses where you've lived before, and what you liked about them…"

"I've always lived in apartments, townhouses, condos."

"Never in a house?" Nikki tried not to sigh. "You've never actually owned property?"

"That's why I want one, you see."

Nikki gave up. "Then let's start by driving past some of the possibilities."

She pushed her chair back and reluctantly looked down at the blanket spread behind her desk. Anna had been asleep for half an hour—not long enough, in Nikki's experience, to take the edge off a cranky baby. But maybe she'd be lucky and the baby would sleep through being picked up and put in the car…

And maybe, she told herself, *silent movies will come back into style, and Neil Hamilton will move to Hollywood instead of Kansas City and I won't have to find him a house after all.*

But Nikki wasn't going to put any money on either bet.

*   *   *

It was dark when she dropped Neil at the real-estate office where he'd left his car all day, and for a couple of minutes she just sat in the parking lot, rolling her head to try to loosen the muscles in her neck. In eight hours she'd managed to change four diapers and feed Anna lunch and a snack, while showing six houses in six separate neighborhoods and driving by seven more. If she hadn't actually done it, she would have sworn it was impossible.

She gave up on the neck exercises and reached for her cell phone. Laura's number rang and rang, and finally the answering machine kicked on. "Seth?" she said. "Are you there?"

Finally the phone clicked. "Yeah. What's up?"

Nikki tried not to let her relief show. "I was starting to wonder where you were."

"That makes two of us. I was under the dishwasher. Where have you been?"

"I thought you said the dishwasher was hopeless. Never mind, you can tell me later. I've been showing houses—what did you think I was doing?"

"I was starting to wonder if you'd gone out dancing with the tycoon."

"Well, he did invite me to dinner. You could have called my cell phone."

"I forgot to ask you for the number."

"Oh—I guess that makes us even, because I don't have yours either. Laura's phone list is posted on the refrigerator door."

"Perfectly sensible," Seth muttered. "Why hang it right next to the phone when it can be all the way across the room?"

"Ask Laura. I thought I'd pick up a pizza. Is pepperoni and extra cheese all right with you?"

"My favorite. And you told me we didn't have anything in common... I thought the tycoon took you to dinner."

"I said he invited me. I'll be home as soon as the pizza's done." Nikki clicked off the phone and sat still for a moment longer. *I'll be home...* It was a good thing Seth hadn't picked up on that little slip, or he'd be tying his jogging shoes right now in an effort to get away from the barest hint of domesticity.

If it hadn't been for the requirement of basic good manners, Nikki would have eaten her share of the pizza on the drive home. Even Anna seemed to perk up at the sharp scent of pepperoni and tomato sauce; the child who had gone as limp as a boneless chicken in protest at being taken in and out of her car seat all day was suddenly sitting up straight and sniffing hungrily.

"Don't get any ideas about snitching my pepperoni," Nikki said. "You're having spaghetti and meatballs. Remember? You heard me order it."

She carried Anna into the house first, and stopped dead just inside the back door. The galley kitchen was completely blocked, with the dishwasher sitting squarely in the center of the narrow walkway.

She took a second look and saw that there were now two dishwashers—the old one blocking the kitchen, and a new one which stuck halfway out of the cabinets.

"Laura will love this setup," she said. "Having to climb over the dishwasher to get to the back door, I mean."

"Sorry." Seth sounded distracted. "I was going to take that out of the way before you got here."

"No problem. You can either let me hand Anna to you, or go open the front door and I'll walk around."

He dusted his hands on his jeans and took the baby. Zack came around the corner on hands and knees, and Anna leaned out of Seth's arms and shrieked, "Kick!"

Nikki snapped her fingers. "So that's what she means! She's been saying it all day. I was starting to think I had a budding soccer star on my hands, when all she wanted was to know where her brother was." She looked past Anna, who was hugging Zack, and gasped.

A narrow red streak scarred the baby's face—running across his forehead, down one cheek, and under the chin. It looked as if he'd been slashed with a razor.

Nikki clutched her chest. "What happened to Zack?"

"Don't panic. It's not permanent. Well, actually, it *was* a permanent marker that he got hold of, but I'm sure it'll wash off sooner or later."

"You gave him a *permanent marker* to play with?"

"I certainly did not. And I didn't give him the brand-new and expensive building permit that he scribbled all over, either."

Nikki winced. "I bet that hurt."

"He's lucky to be here. Between the building permit and the client he hung up on—"

Nikki put both hands up, palms out. "Hold the fort for a minute, I'm going after the pizza. I suspect I'm going to need fuel to listen to this story."

When she came back with the boxes, he'd shifted the dishwasher enough that she could squeeze by. She set the pizza on the counter, got two plates down from the cabinet, and opened the order of spaghetti and meatballs, cutting the meat into twin-sized bites. It was a mindless chore, and her attention drifted to a slip of paper on the counter. "I had no idea dishwashers cost that much," she said.

Seth shot her a sideways look and slid the receipt out from under the pizza box. It vanished into his pocket with the same smoothness that a magician would use to make a white rabbit disappear.

Thoughtfully, Nikki continued to mince meatballs. "Did Laura call today?"

"No. Why?"

"I thought maybe you'd have talked to her before you spent that much money on a new dishwasher."

Nikki thought for a minute that he wasn't going to answer at all, but finally Seth said, "I'm going to tell her it was left over from a job. Was the tycoon up to your expectations?"

"Oh, quite." She kept her tone airy.

"Then why didn't you go to dinner with him?"

She gave it up. "Because eight hours in one day is all I could take," she admitted.

"You do that a lot with guys, don't you?"

"What do you mean?"

"Well, the stockbroker bored you, and now the tycoon."

"There is no comparison. I have to listen to Neil Hamilton. Which reminds me..."

"I don't think I like the sound of this."

"About tomorrow, Seth..."

He ran a hand through his hair. "Not on your life. One more day with Zack in tow and I won't have a business left."

"No, no. It's only the evening. Neil has meetings all day."

"Wait a minute. I thought you weren't going out with him."

"I'm not. We still have houses to look at."

"Eight hours and he couldn't find anything he liked?"

"Some people buy the first thing they look at. Others want to check out everything before they decide."

And some of them are more interested in looking than buying. Nikki was beginning to think Bryan had been right when he'd called Neil Hamilton a tourist. Not that she'd admit it to Bryan—or for that matter, to Seth.

"If you'll keep the twins in the evening," she went on, "I can finish off the list with him. It won't take nearly as long if I'm not dragging Anna in and out of the car at every stop."

"Or trying to keep Zack from eating grass," Seth said absently. "And then you'll be done?"

"For this round, anyway. He's flying back to Detroit Thursday morning." She set the twins' plates in the dining room and scooped up Zack to put him in his high chair. "Seth, after the first couple of houses, he actually suggested that I just leave Anna sitting in the car while we looked around. Come on, I have to do this. Help me. Please."

He captured Anna, who protested at being picked up but sniffed thoughtfully as he set the plate of spaghetti on the tray in front of her.

Nikki put a slice of pizza on a plate and handed it to Seth.

"On one condition," he said.

She paused in midmotion. "What's that?"

"Hey, you're not in much of a position to bargain, you know. After tomorrow, we both take the rest of the week off."

"So we don't have to juggle babies? That's not a condition, Seth, that's a reward. I couldn't do that to Anna again, anyway—the poor kid was exhausted from getting in and out of the car all day."

"And you don't look so good, either."

"My back aches," Nikki admitted. "That's a pretty awkward angle to be lifting twenty pounds, especially when she doesn't want to be lifted."

He set the pizza plate down and moved around behind

her, his hands warm against her shoulder blades. "Tell me where it hurts."

"All over."

He pulled out a chair. "Here. Sit down backwards and fold your arms on the back. It's a pretty makeshift massage bench, but it works in a pinch."

Nikki sat down, propped her chin on her hands, and sagged. No wonder Anna had done the limp-chicken act, she thought—it felt good to pretend to be boneless.

She noticed that Zack had given up on his spoon and was feeding himself spaghetti by the fistful, but she couldn't muster up enough energy to care. He wasn't going to starve, and at the moment that was the only thing which mattered. In fact, now that he was half-covered in marinara sauce, the red marker hardly showed at all.

Seth used his thumbs to massage her spinal column and the flat of his hands to rub the sore spots across her shoulders. When he moved up her neck, using his fingertips to work the muscles, Nikki groaned. He froze, and she said, "Don't stop. That feels so good."

She lifted a hand and pulled the clip out of her hair, releasing the twist at the back of her head so he could more easily run his fingers over her scalp. "You're handy to have around, you know that?" she asked lazily. "You'd better watch out or some woman's going to try to keep you."

He stopped rubbing. For an instant, he was absolutely still. Nikki felt as if his fingertips were electrical contacts and her scalp a transformer. *Idiot*, she told herself. *Don't act domestic—even if it's the farthest thing from your mind, you can't afford for him to get the wrong idea. You need him. The kids need him.*

And even though she'd like him to keep on rubbing her back for the next year, it was time to call a halt. She pushed herself up from the chair and turned with what she hoped was only a comradely smile. "Thanks, Seth. That felt wonderful. Hey, what happened to your neck?"

He ran a finger down his throat, tracing the scratch. "Zack was making a point. It won't happen again, because I trimmed his fingernails while he was napping this afternoon."

"Good thinking." She got herself a piece of pizza and reached into the refrigerator for a soda. "Here's my cell number if you want it, by the way." She ran a finger down the phone list, looking for his, and knocked loose the magnet which held the list onto the refrigerator door. As she grabbed for the magnet, a slip of paper fluttered out of the calendar which was stuck up next to the list.

She muttered under her breath and picked it up from the floor. She'd actually stuck it back on the refrigerator before her tired brain registered what it was. "Oh, no," she whispered.

"What now?" Seth asked warily.

"Tomorrow's Wednesday the fifth—right?"

"Yeah. Why?"

"Because this is an appointment card. *'Twins' portrait, Jensen Studio, Wednesday, September fifth, 10:00 a.m.'*" She looked up at Seth. "Now what do we do?"

CHAPTER FIVE

NIKKI was startled when Seth shrugged the problem off as no big deal. "Getting their picture taken can be the adventure of the day for the three of you," he said.

It would be an adventure, all right. Nikki's head was swimming at the very thought of dressing up two babies and getting them to sit up straight and smile—at the exact same moment the camera clicked. She'd rather go into a circus ring with a couple of tigers. At least the cats were trained to follow commands.

"And with Zack's face looking as if he's been slashed in a gang war," she said dryly, "I'm sure it'll be a portrait that Laura will want to hang over prominently over the fireplace, too."

Seth's forehead wrinkled. "What fireplace?"

"In their next house."

"They're looking for another house?"

"Stop changing the subject," Nikki ordered.

"I'm not even the one who brought up—oh, all right." He took a deep breath and blew it out with a whoosh. "I'd forgotten about Zack's face," he admitted. "I guess I don't want that immortalized on film."

He looked so chagrined that Nikki forgave him. "If you can scrub him off before Laura gets home, she'll never have to know what happened."

The corner of his mouth turned up. "Are you offering to share secrets with me, Nikki?"

"No—I'm collecting blackmail material on you. Not that I think I'll have to keep that promise not to tell his mom, because it would take sandpaper to clean him up enough to fool her.''

Seth looked thoughtful. "What about one of those spa places? Somebody was telling me they promise to shave years from your age by taking off the top layer of skin. What do they call that? Skin peels?''

"Face peels." Nikki wondered which of the blond models would have been dumb enough to tell him about face peels. *Wrong question,* she thought. *Which one would be smart enough not to?* "That would be worse than the sandpaper.''

Seth looked a bit disappointed.

"Even if it wasn't for Zack's face, though, we couldn't do it—I have no idea how Laura wants them dressed, or—'' She saw him start to open his mouth and added, "Don't tell me one outfit is just as good as another, either, because it's not.''

"You're the expert on making things look good, Nikki. Though I was just thinking we could leave him this way. By tomorrow morning the spaghetti sauce will have hardened and it'll cover up everything underneath, so Laura would never know the difference. No? All right. Call the studio and cancel the appointment.''

"It's too late tonight. I'll phone early in the morning.'' She looked at the card again. "I hope rescheduling is no big thing. This says Laura's already paid for the sitting.''

"They must do it all the time,'' Seth said. "Would you stop worrying about it and help excavate the kids from the spaghetti so you can give them a bath?''

"Why is the bath my job? I thought this was a partnership.''

"I still have to finish the dishwasher. Unless of course you want to walk around it all day tomorrow. Or I can leave you the installation guide so you can—''

"Get to work," Nikki ordered.

The only clean spots she could find on the babies were the seat of their pants and the small circle where their bibs had protected their shirts, so she filled the basin with cold water and started dumping every item of clothing in as she removed it. If she was lucky, the tomato stains would soak out. And heaven knew she was due for a little good fortune—she'd had her share of the other kind.

She put Anna in the tub and chased Zack down to strip off his tiny jeans, and her eyebrows raised at what she found underneath. By the time both babies were clean, diapered and pajama-clad, she was pretty well covered with tomato sauce herself, so she put on her sweats and submerged her tailored pinstriped shirt in the cold water as well. Then she had to pursue both the babies into the living room, where they'd scampered in order to avoid being put to bed.

"You'd increase your odds of success," she told them as she scooped them up, "if you went in opposite directions. On second thought, forget I said that."

By the time they were settled, Nikki felt as if the circus ring full of tigers would have been a much easier way to spend the evening.

Seth was lying on his back under the sink, doing something to the drain. The old dishwasher was gone from the center of the room, but everything Laura had stored in the cabinets was stacked helter-skelter on the floor by the back door.

Nikki leaned against the counter and contemplated the mess. "I don't suppose you'd like to tell me why Zack was wearing a strip of duct tape under his clothes."

Seth was matter-of-fact. "He was wiggling so much that I couldn't get his diaper on tight enough. So I pulled it apart to try again, and then the sticky tabs wouldn't work."

"So you patched his diaper together with duct tape?"

"It was the only thing I could reach at the time."

Nikki told herself not to ask, but the words came out anyway. "Do I want to know where you were doing this?"

"On a portable workbench, and he was eyeing the router and a jigsaw and trying to decide which one to grab for first."

Nikki winced at the thought.

"Hey, it stayed on," Seth pointed out.

"Yeah. In fact, it stayed on so well I had to find a pair of scissors to get it off."

"Don't blame me. They should make those fastener things stronger."

Nikki rolled her eyes.

"I stuck the pizza in the oven to warm it up."

In all the confusion, Nikki had almost forgotten the pizza and how hungry she'd been. In fact, she hadn't even managed a bite for herself. She picked up the can of soda she'd opened earlier. It had gone flat, but she took a gulp anyway.

Seth twisted a handle under the sink. "If this connection just doesn't leak, the job's finished."

"Great timing," Nikki said. "I bet you've just been lying there taking it easy while I fought the battle of the bath."

"Want to switch places? It's not exactly a featherbed."

She took a second look and decided that the cabinet's edge must be cutting painfully into his shoulder blades. She shook her head and changed the subject in order to distract herself from the idea of Seth in a featherbed. "Laura will worship you for this. Tell me again how you're going to explain it to her."

"Why do you want to know?"

"So I don't slip up and give you away." Nikki's voice

was tart. "Goodness knows you wouldn't want to get a reputation for generosity."

"No," Seth said softly. "What I don't want is to make Laura feel like a charity case."

Nikki bit her lip. She should have seen that herself, of course. Asking him to work on the dishwasher at all must have been difficult enough for Laura, but accepting the gift of a new one—admitting that she and Stephen couldn't afford it on their own—would be more than she could bear. "You actually expect her to believe that someone discarded a brand-new dishwasher?"

"*Almost* brand-new. I'll tell her we're installing a new kitchen in Mission Hills—that much is true—and let her draw her own conclusions."

"Oh, in that case, she'll believe it," Nikki said. "I sold a house out there last year. It brought well over a million dollars, but the new owner never even went inside. He just sent in a bulldozer to knock it down so he could build the house he really wanted."

"Exactly. A guy like that—or his wife—wouldn't think twice about discarding a dishwasher just because the buttons weren't in the right place."

A phone buzzed. Nikki reached for her pocket and remembered that she'd changed clothes—her phone was still in her jacket in the bedroom. "That must be yours. Want me to get it?"

"It's in my toolbox, if you'll hand it to me."

He couldn't make it plainer that he didn't want her to answer it. Well, that made sense, Nikki thought. It was probably one of his blond models, and he didn't want to explain why there was a woman answering his phone. *Like I'd want to chat with one of them.*

She dug the phone out of the box and handed it over without a word.

"Yeah?" Seth said. "Well, not at the moment. Are you going to be at home? I'm in a bit of an awkward position right now."

Nikki wondered whether he meant the fact that he was lying under a sink, or that there was another woman in the room where she could listen to the conversation.

Don't be silly, she told herself. *He wouldn't let your presence stop him from saying whatever he wanted, because you don't begin to count as another woman in his eyes.*

"Yeah, I had fun, too. Look, I'll call you later." Seth snapped the phone closed.

Nikki had to bite her tongue to keep from suggesting that—judging by the absent-minded tone of his voice—the occasion didn't sound as if it had been the world's most successful date. But commenting would only make it clear that she had indeed been listening, and perhaps leave the impression that she cared who he talked to and what he said.

So she stuck a fingernail under a label on the edge of the dishwasher door and pulled the corner loose. "If you're going to tell Laura that this isn't quite new," she pointed out, "you might want to peel all the stickers off."

"Looks like you're doing fine." Seth hauled himself out from under the sink. "But hand me that wrench, and I'll put a dent in the front panel just to make it more convincing."

"Let's not go to extremes."

He grinned. "Then give me all the stuff from under the sink and I'll put it back in."

Nikki began passing him bins and buckets. When everything was stowed away once more, Seth stood up and stretched. "I'm glad to be out of there. Here's the real challenge.'' He started pushing buttons, and water surged into the dishwasher.

"Hey, why waste the opportunity?" Nikki waved a hand at the dishes stacked in the sink.

"I don't want to complicate things at the moment, just check out the cycle. Besides, the pizza should be hot again by now. Let's eat."

The cheese had gone rubbery from being reheated, and the crust was a bit limp, but it still tasted good. Nikki collapsed on the couch with a plate and put her feet up.

Seth carried the pizza box in and sank down beside her. "Are you ticklish?" he asked.

"What?"

"I was just continuing the likes and dislikes game, and I wondered if—"

"If I was, I wouldn't tell you."

"That must mean you are, because otherwise you'd have just said you weren't. So we both like pepperoni and we're both ticklish. And there's always your ex-fiancé," Seth added helpfully. "That's something we have in common."

Nikki couldn't help it. She let her eyes widen till they must look as if they were ready to pop out, and she forced a breathless note into her voice. "You mean you were engaged to Thorpe, too? Seth, I had no idea—"

"It's a shame I wasn't," he said lightly. "I'd have thought far enough ahead to keep the diamond instead of throwing it at him."

Nikki shrugged. She wasn't about to explain to Seth what she'd been thinking when she'd flung her engagement ring in Thorpe's face. For that matter, she wasn't sure she could explain it to herself—or even remember the details.

"What ever happened to him, anyway?" Seth asked.

"He moved to California. At least that's what one of the bridesmaids told me."

"He couldn't stand the heat here, huh?"

Nikki remembered what Seth had said about admiring her for facing the crowd on her wedding day, despite the embarrassment of admitting that she wasn't going to be married after all. "I don't think it was that, because his friends thought he was pretty macho. For months I heard about how unreasonable I was being to hold it against him, how it wasn't his fault, that he hadn't hired the call girls—oh, all right, exotic dancers—for the bachelor party."

"They just showed up?"

"It doesn't sound very likely, does it?" Idly, she rolled her pizza slice up till it looked vaguely like an egg roll, and nibbled the end of it. "Anyway, I gave the ring back because I didn't want to keep anything that would remind me of him."

"That's a polite way to tell me to stop talking about it, right?"

"Congratulations. You win the grand prize—the last slice of pizza."

"You're sure you don't want it?"

"I can't eat another thing. If you're finished playing with the dishwasher, I'll load it up and give it a real test."

"I'll get it later. Go to bed—you look beat."

Nikki couldn't decide whether to be grateful or insulted. As she was pulling back the comforter, she began to wonder how Seth had managed the night before. It must have been chilly with only the crocheted throw that Laura always left draped over the back of the couch. And since the little house had no official linen closet, the extra blankets and pillows were stored in the top of the closet in the master bedroom. She got out one of each and took them out to the living room.

From the kitchen she heard the rumble of Seth's voice, punctuated with the rattle of dishes. It was odd that she'd never noticed before how low and rich his voice was. Strange how hearing someone without being able to see them made such a difference in perceptions...

Or maybe, she told herself, it wasn't odd at all. She hadn't noticed before because he probably only sounded that way when he was chatting up Elsa or Inga or whatever the current blonde's name was, and not when he talked to Nikki.

Though the pillow and blanket helped, Seth woke up again with a stiff neck and a sore shoulder. In fact, every joint in his body felt absolutely creaky, and he almost limped into the babies' room, where Zack was lying on his tummy in his crib, yelping like a puppy and stretching one hand through the bars as far as he could in order to jab Anna awake.

"Knock it off, pal," Seth warned. "Take a lesson—waking a woman up in the morning before she's ready is the worst single thing a guy can do."

Zack crowed happily and pulled himself up till he was standing in his crib.

"And that comes from somebody who knows what he's talking about," Nikki added from behind him. "Though his experience may only apply to blondes."

Seth glanced over his shoulder. She was still wearing her sweats, there wasn't a drop of makeup on her face, and she'd pulled her hair up into a careless ponytail. She looked about sixteen. "Is that an offer? Because—in the name of science—I should take any opportunity for further study in order to test my hypothesis."

She tipped her head to one side and studied him. "Sure," she said. "When you wake up tomorrow morning—on the couch—pop on in and see whether I bite your head off. In the meantime, I'll leave you two gentlemen to theorize about it.''

"She doesn't sound sixteen, does she?'' Seth asked, under his breath.

Zack giggled and held up his arms to be lifted out of the crib.

When Seth reached the kitchen, carrying a baby under each arm, Nikki was pacing the floor with the phone tucked under her chin.

"I understand that you have a policy,'' she said, and it was apparent to Seth that she was holding on to her temper with a leash. "I'm telling you that no matter what your policy is, it's impossible for us to keep the appointment this morning. We're talking about babies here. Children get sick, they get hurt…'' She stopped pacing and closed her eyes, listening. "No, not sick exactly, but—''

Seth stopped listening and started mixing cereal. He was feeding the babies by the time Nikki put the phone down with a bang. "That is the most ridiculous thing I've ever heard,'' she stormed. "How they can stay in business with that policy is beyond me.''

"No changes, no refunds?'' Seth guessed.

She assumed a whiny, nasal tone. "'We never give refunds. We can schedule a later date if you're willing to pay a second fee, but we only change an appointment without charge if we're given at least a day's notice. That's because if someone cancels at the last moment like this, we can't fill that slot again.' Can you believe it?''

Seth handed her a spoon. "Make yourself useful.''

Mechanically she began feeding Anna. "It's not a bad business plan, you know—collect the full fee but don't do the work. You wouldn't even need to own a camera, just hire a snippy little receptionist and teach her to keep saying 'time is money' till the customer either screams or gives up.''

"Which must mean you're not giving up, because you were certainly screaming.''

"I do not scream on the phone,'' Nikki said with dignity. "Honestly, how do they get by with this? Where would I be if I charged people when they didn't show up for their appointments to look at houses? Where would you be if you charged potential clients for every job you estimated but didn't actually get?''

"You mean, besides being a lot richer?''

"From the fees, maybe—if we could collect them. But we'd both be without a single real customer.'' She slammed the spoon down on the high chair tray. Anna jumped and looked at her, wide-eyed. "That's it. I'm going over there to give them a piece of my mind.''

"Forget it, Nikki. How much can another sitting cost? It's worth the price not to have to dress up two kids and get all the way over to the mall by ten o'clock.''

"It's not the money, it's the principle. Besides, the studio is at the mall and there's a supermarket right there—I can pick up the groceries we need, too.'' She was still talking to herself as she went off toward the bedroom.

"Whoops,'' Seth said. *Time for some fast action.* He snatched the spoons from the babies' hands and set them aside, reaching for a washcloth instead. Anna, who had her mouth open for the next bite, gave an unhappy little yowl as he picked her up.

He was in the babies' room when Nikki came out in jeans and a sweater, tucking her wallet and cell phone into her pockets. "I'll be back just as soon as I can, so I won't hold you up from going to work.'' She paused. "What are you doing?''

Seth fitted a small arm into a sleeve and said, "I'm getting the babies ready to go with you."

"I'm not taking the babies. That's—"

"—The only way you'll possibly convince that receptionist, or her boss, to give you a break."

"I suppose you're right," she said slowly.

"Of course I'm right. There's no point in pushing it. Let them be stubborn and lose customers. What difference does it make to you?"

Nikki shook her head. "I feel very strongly about this. They're taking advantage of people like Laura, and I don't like it."

"Okay," Seth said and picked up a tiny pair of denim overalls. "It's your funeral, though, because the twins didn't finish breakfast."

He thought she looked a little doubtful at that news, but then her pointed little chin set firmly. "Dammit, Seth, somebody's got to stand up to them." She reached for a matching shirt and the other baby.

He helped her manipulate the twins and their stroller down the front steps and around to the driveway, and watched her look from the stroller to the infinitesimal trunk of her car. He wondered if she realized how helpless she looked when she chewed on her lower lip like that. Not that he was going to point it out to her, because he figured the ever-resourceful, stand-on-her-own Nikki Marshall wouldn't appreciate hearing that she looked like a waif sometimes. A charming, sexy waif—but still a waif.

He popped the back hatch of his SUV and lifted the stroller in. "Come on. I'll get Anna's car seat."

Relief made her eyes sparkle like amber, and the smile she gave him made the sun look dim. If it hadn't been for the alarm bells going off in his brain, it might have been fun to watch her. Maybe even nudge her along and see how far she'd go in trying to enchant him.

"Hey," he said lightly. "Lay off, okay? You're making me dizzy. The truth is I wouldn't miss this encounter for the world."

It was a couple of minutes before ten when they reached the photography studio, just off the center courtyard of the mall. The business was already open, its metal gates pushed back to leave the entire storefront open to the walkway. The waiting room was lined with wall-sized portraits of children. "Baby!" Anna announced, pointing to a picture of a child at least twice as old as she was. Zack seemed fascinated by the rainbow of colors in a gum ball machine which stood just outside the studio. For the moment, miraculously, neither of them was trying to escape the stroller.

In a kiosk in one corner, two women sat. One must be the receptionist she'd talked to earlier, Nikki thought. The other was a customer who was trying to decide which picture package to order, but who was constantly being distracted by a three-year-old who was carrying toys over to show her. Nearby sat a woman with three small girls who were wearing identical red velvet dresses in stair-step sizes.

Nikki strolled over to the reception desk and stood tapping her fingers gently on the counter. "By the time she finishes with the customer, I suppose she'll tell us we're too late for our appointment," she said under her breath.

There was no answer from Seth. Puzzled, she turned around and gasped. Seth, stroller, babies and all, had disappeared without a noise, even a whimper.

It's hardly likely they've been kidnapped, Nikki told herself. *Maybe they're just around the other side of the gum ball machine, learning their colors.*

Before she could quite convince herself, she saw Seth

pushing the stroller toward her from the food court just down the hallway. Of course, she thought. He hadn't had time for breakfast either. It was silly to feel relieved.

Then she realized that he wasn't holding anything, but the twins were. Each of them was using both small hands to grip what looked like—

"Ice cream cones?" Nikki said. "Have you lost your bloomin' mind?"

Seth looked mildly surprised. "I warned you that they didn't finish breakfast."

"Strawberry ice cream is not an appropriate breakfast food."

"There's protein in milk, isn't there? And strawberries are fruit."

"They can't chew up a cone!"

"I'll watch them." His voice dropped. "Besides, the studio will be so anxious to get rid of the pair of them before they smear up all the other clients that they'll give you whatever you want."

Nikki stared at him. Then she glanced over her shoulder at the mother of three, who had drawn her velvet-dressed daughters close. There was a look of horror on the woman's face, and Nikki didn't blame her. From the corner of her eye she could see Anna's cone slowly tipping to the side.

"That's either the smartest idea I've ever heard, or the craziest," Nikki said.

The customer in the kiosk pointed toward them and said something to the receptionist, who looked across at the twins and jumped to her feet.

"Go get 'em, honey," Seth said. "I'll just stand back here and watch the fireworks."

But the woman didn't approach Nikki. Instead, she vanished through a door into the back of the studio. Her voice drifted back to the waiting room. Though Nikki couldn't make out the words, the woman's tone made her irritation clear. Nikki took a deep breath.

Half a minute later a man emerged, looking exasperated. "What is going on out here?" he demanded, waving the camera he was holding. "I'm in the middle of a sitting and my receptionist tells me...oh, my goodness."

Nikki followed his gaze. Anna had shifted her misshapen, soggy cone into her right hand, holding it in a Statue-of-Liberty pose, and she was using her left hand to brace herself so she could lean across the stroller and take a lick from Zack's cone. Pink droplets formed a chain over her chin and down her forearm from her own treat. Zack looked as if he was thinking about shoving the rest of his ice cream up her nose. His own face was so covered that the red marker barely showed.

"Seth," Nikki said. "Take them out to the hallway, please. Quickly, before they drip all over the carpet."

"No!" the photographer said. "No, don't move anything!" He raised the camera and began to snap—moving, crouching, twisting. Apparently fascinated by his gyrations, the twins sat with eyes wide and only their tongues moving, both still taking an occasional swipe at Zack's cone. Anna's forgotten one tipped further in her hand, and a blob of ice cream plopped onto the floor.

The photographer sighed with what sounded like satisfaction. "That's going to be a prize-winning photo," he said softly, and his gaze snapped to Nikki. "You can look at proofs next week. There will be no charge for shooting the pictures." He sounded as if he thought he was doing her a major favor.

Nikki's jaw dropped. He would even *consider* charging a fee for this?

He added slyly, "That is, if you'll sign a release so I can

use the photos in contests. Maybe in ads as well. It could even get them started as models.''

Nikki took a second to recover her poise. ''I'm afraid I can't sign anything,'' she said sweetly, ''because they're not my children.''

He looked quickly at Seth, who shook his head. ''Not mine, either.''

The photographer's face drooped like a basset hound's.

''But I'll tell you what,'' Nikki said. ''If you make an exception to your policy about rescheduling appointments and let my friend bring her babies in to get a real picture taken at her convenience, I can probably persuade her to sign the paperwork you need.''

''Any time,'' the photographer said quickly. ''It would make an even better photograph than this if I had them dressed up and under the lights before we give them the ice cream.''

Nikki opened her mouth, gulped, and closed it again.

It took a bit of persuasion to convince the babies to relinquish the sodden cones, and some time to mop up the mess. On the way to the car, Nikki shot a look at Seth, who was obviously having trouble keeping a straight face.

''All right, go ahead and say it,'' she challenged. ''You were right. I should have left it alone. I'll just pay for another sitting—somewhere else—and pretend this never happened.''

''And forget about this set of proofs?'' he said mildly. ''They'll be ready next week.''

''You think I'm going to tell Laura about this so-called sitting? She'd kill me.''

''Then I'll come and choose the best ones. I'm going to want one for my desk, one on my bedside table, one in my car and a couple for my wallet. Maybe one on the bathroom mirror. Oh, and the refrigerator door. Hell, I'll just take one of each.''

Nikki couldn't help smiling. Whatever he might say, he was obviously attached to the babies—in fact, the perfect uncle. ''That's so sweet. They are going to be cute pictures, aren't they?—even if Laura would hate them.''

''Cute has nothing to do with it,'' Seth said. ''I'm only interested in self-preservation.''

''What are you talking about?''

''If I have the reminders of this week staring at me anywhere I look,'' he said grimly, ''I'll never get myself into this situation again.''

CHAPTER SIX

HIS words seemed to ring in Nikki's head. *I'll never get myself into this situation again,* Seth had said.

Well, Nikki thought, that certainly let her know where she stood...

Hold it a minute, she told herself. *And exactly which part of that didn't you already know?*

Seth had made it quite clear from the beginning that it was only his sense of responsibility toward his brother's twins which was keeping him involved here. As far as that was concerned, Nikki had to agree—fond as she was of the babies, if she'd had any idea she was signing up for a week of full-time duty instead of just a few days, she'd have run for the hills rather than volunteering.

And as for the idea that Seth helping out had anything to do with being interested in Nikki herself...only a fool would think that there was anything to that.

And only a fool would want to, she told herself briskly.

This whole experience was obviously softening her brain. The sooner Laura got home, the sooner Nikki got back to her regular routine, and the sooner Seth got back to his blondes, the better it would be for all of them.

"Do you have a favorite supermarket, or will any one of them do?" Seth asked.

Nikki had to pull herself back to the present. "Oh—right, the groceries. Never mind—I'll take care of that later. You must be anxious to get to work."

"Not particularly," he said dryly. "Everybody's going to be upset with me today."

So that was why he'd really come along. Not to give her a hand; not even because he expected to be amused by the confrontation in the photo studio, but simply because he didn't want to go to work.

Don't take it personally, she told herself. Given the choice between going to the mall with Seth and the twins or showing Neil Hamilton half a dozen more houses, she'd take the mall over going to work, too.

She kept her voice light. "Why? Is it the client Zack hung up on that you're avoiding, or the one whose building permit he scribbled all over?"

"Oh, nuts, I'd forgotten about the building permit."

"Well, if it's still readable, maybe it won't matter."

"Let's hope so, or when he's thirty he'll be still doing odd jobs to work off the extra fees."

Nikki tried to smother a grin. That was pretty obviously an idle threat, coming from the same guy who'd figured out a way to give Laura a new dishwasher without making her feel patronized. "That might actually please his mother."

"Because he'll have a guaranteed job?"

"And she won't have to worry about building a college fund for him, if he'll be too busy picking up nails and emptying trash to go to school."

"I'll keep that in mind. Do you want me to move the car seats or leave you the SUV?"

Nikki raised her eyebrows. "You'd actually trust me with your car again?"

"Only because it's pretty difficult to get myself far enough into yours to tighten things down."

He could just dump the seats in the driveway and tell her to take care of it herself. But he hadn't. *Of course, he wants the twins to be safe.*

"You really are a nice guy, you know," Nikki said. "Do

you suppose when all this is over, we can actually be friends?''

She thought for a few seconds that he hadn't heard her.

"Sure," he said finally. "I suppose we could even double-date."

"I don't think—" Nikki swallowed the rest of the sentence. It probably wasn't smart to invite a guy to be a friend and then in the next breath insult his taste in women. Not that he didn't already know what she thought of his girlfriends anyway, so there was really no point in saying it again. But if he thought there was the slightest chance that she'd get chummy with an Inga or an Elsa....

"Not precisely what you had in mind?" Seth shot a look at her. "So what were you thinking about, Nikki?"

She'd never felt so awkward in her life. It was true that she hadn't been picturing them as part of a foursome—but if she said anything of the kind, he was likely to leap to the conclusion that she was suggesting a date...

Well? she asked herself. *Exactly what are you suggesting, Nikki Marshall?* "Just...you know...friends," she said. "Oh, forget it. I wasn't thinking, exactly."

"Exactly," he repeated, not quite under his breath.

Nikki was a bit irritated. Did he have to take everything so personally? *So much for the nice guy.*

He backed the SUV into the drive and got the stroller out while Nikki retrieved the twins. Next door, a gray-haired woman in a housecoat opened her front door and reached for the newspaper which was lying on the welcome mat. "Good morning," she called. "You're out early today, Mrs. Baxter."

Nikki shot a look at Seth, but in his struggle to unfold the stroller he apparently wasn't listening. *So do I just say Hi and let it go at that?* Nikki wondered. *Or correct her?*

The woman squinted and frowned. "No, wait a minute.

You're not Mrs. Baxter. How did I possibly mistake you for her? Her hair isn't nearly as red as yours. Did you buy the Baxters' house? But those are her babies—aren't they?''

Seth pushed the stroller up beside the SUV and took Zack from Nikki's arms. ''Yes, their parents threw them in with the house,'' he said under his breath. ''The deal includes washer, dryer, drapes, twins…''

Nikki was so relieved that he apparently wasn't going to have an attack over the mistaken identification that she started to giggle. ''We're just taking care of them for a few days,'' she called.

''So much for asking her to baby-sit,'' Seth muttered. ''And here I was thinking we might have stumbled onto a solution.''

To say that no one was going to be particularly happy with him today had been an understatement, Seth realized within a few minutes of reaching Emily Cooper's new addition. Two of his workmen were getting ready to drill holes in the existing concrete wall around the soon-to-be-ex-window, so the gap could be filled and properly supported with reinforcing rod. A third was scouting out scrap boards to build forms to hold the new pour in place while it dried. Two more were setting up the concrete saw they would need to cut a hole in the wall around the corner, where the new window would face out over Emily Cooper's own back lawn instead of her neighbor's.

In short the entire crew was tied up with Emily's Cooper's change order, and it appeared to Seth as if they hadn't accomplished much all morning.

The foreman snapped a case of drill bits closed and glowered at him. ''Want to explain to me again why we're doing this, boss?''

Seth didn't bother. "I thought you'd be well along with the job by now."

"We've been stalling till you showed up, hoping that you'd just lost your mind yesterday and you'd get it back by this morning and tell us not to go ahead."

Seth waved a hand at the guys running the cement saw. They pulled protective earmuffs and goggles into place and started up the motor, and with a shriek like a thousand banshees the saw blade bit slowly into the wall.

Seth winced. As often as he had listened to a concrete saw, he would never get used to the screech of the blade, high-pitched and eerie. He stepped outside the addition, where the sound wasn't quite as obnoxiously loud. "It's probably a good thing you didn't start this a few hours ago," he observed to the foreman. "The neighbors would have been pitching golf clubs and rotten tomatoes at you."

"You think we're nuts?" the foreman said with a growl and moved off to help construct the forms.

Gradually, centimeter by centimeter, the blade chewed and a dust cloud formed around the saw. From the corner of his eye, Seth caught a glimpse of something pink and fluffy, and he turned to see Emily Cooper coming around the side of the house, wearing a ruffled chiffon house coat. She looked as if she'd just climbed out of bed, though— despite her garb—her very-black hair was already carefully coiffed. Or perhaps, he thought, it was just sprayed to such a glassy finish that not even lying down could flatten it. And she had either paused long enough to put on makeup before she came outside, or she'd had her eyeliner tattooed in place. He was willing to bet it was the permanent kind, just as he'd have staked his SUV that she'd had at least two facelifts. Emily, he estimated, was a good fifteen years older than she admitted.

This morning, she was carrying her poodle. One ring-bedecked hand supported the tiny dog's stomach, the other was cupped over the poodle's topknot in an effort to cover both ears. Emily Cooper was obviously yelling something; Seth could see her lips moving, but he couldn't make out the words.

He waved down the foreman, who strolled over to the men running the saw. They cut the motor and the sound faded, though it seemed to echo round the inside of the addition for half a minute even after he knew the saw had gone silent.

"What is that racket?" Emily Cooper asked angrily.

"We're moving your window, as you requested."

"Well, can't you do it quietly? You woke me up, you've upset my dog, you've got the neighborhood in an up-roar—"

"I did warn you," Seth reminded, "that moving the window would be expensive and messy."

"You didn't warn me that it would be noisier than an atomic blast," she said irritably.

There was no doubt in Seth's mind that he'd told her about the noise. Of course, until someone had actually heard a concrete saw running, they usually had a different definition of noise.

She really did look frazzled. The dog looked even worse, when it came right down to it. "We can hold off for a while if you'd like."

"What difference will that make? It's still going to be as loud."

"I thought you might like to go out for the day and avoid the noise."

Her eyes narrowed. "How long is this going to take?"

Depends on how long you need to get dressed. "We may be done today. But that wall's pretty solid. If you'll recall, that's why you wanted us to build it out of concrete in the first place. You might want to stay in a hotel overnight, just to be on the safe side.''

"What about the neighbors? Two of them have phoned to complain. I can't take them all to a hotel!''

"You could leave the window where you originally wanted it.''

She was obviously weighing the options.

"We could still add a couple of skylights, if we decide before the roof tile goes up,'' Seth offered. "That way, even with blinds closed over the window, you'd get plenty of sunshine into the room.''

He almost held his breath, but the compromise seemed to be just face-saving enough that she could accept it. "Oh, all right,'' she said ungraciously. "But this isn't turning out at all as I expected. And it's taking much longer than I thought it would.''

Changing the plans twice a day isn't helping that, Seth wanted to say.

"My housewarming party is coming up fast, and all you're accomplishing is to make even more of a mess. I hope you're not planning to charge me for repairing the damage your men have done this morning, because it's certainly not my fault that you were too busy with that baby yesterday to tell me exactly what moving the window would be like.''

Whether her complaints were real or not, she obviously needed someone to blame just now, and Seth knew better than to try to correct her. She was already on a roll, and explaining would only increase her fury.

"Well,'' she went on, "as long as you don't have that appendage along to distract you today, there's something else I'd like to point out.''

Appendage. Zack wouldn't know the word, of course, but the baby was no fool—he'd have recognized the tone of Emily Cooper's voice. Just as he had yesterday, when he'd clung to Seth like a newborn monkey.

Emily Cooper went on, "There's a wall I'm just not sure about."

Here we go again, Seth thought. But there was one big difference from yesterday. He was actually feeling lonely for Zack.

Nikki had put on the last clean outfit she possessed, and she was folding laundry in the living room while the twins played on a blanket nearby. The couch was piled with small clothes in neatly folded stacks. Among the tiny jeans and shirts and sleepers and rompers and overalls were a few of her own things—her favorite pinstriped blouse, for one. Despite her best efforts, it was still blotched with the faint orange aftereffects of marinara sauce from the twins' spaghetti spree. Most of the rest of her wardrobe was sadly in need of a visit to the dry cleaner.

There was nothing for it, she thought. She'd have to make a run out to her townhouse for more clothes. At the rate this was going, she thought, she might as well just move everything she owned.

She heard a door slam outside and went to glance out the window into the driveway. Seth's SUV was there, and so was a pickup truck and a couple of guys who were loading Laura's old dishwasher into the back. Only when they drove away did Seth come in.

"Getting rid of the evidence, I see," Nikki said.

"Of course. We'll dispose of it with the regular construction debris. I don't need to keep it because I have you to swear that it wasn't repairable."

"Well, you sound cheerful for a guy who was expecting to be on everybody's hate list today. Or are you just relieved to be done for the day?"

"Done? I thought I was only starting on the real chore."
He ruffled the twins' hair and dropped a bright-colored
plastic ring onto the stacking pole in front of Anna. "Are
you anxious to see the tycoon? Or just anxious to get out
of here?"

"Anxious to have the evening over with." She gathered
up as many stacks of small clothes as she could hold and
took them into the twins' room to put away.

Seth followed with the rest. "Is this guy more annoying
than your usual customer, or are you just edgy because of
the situation?"

Nikki considered. "A little of both, I think. He has no
idea what he wants. He just says that he'll know it when
he sees it."

"So he wants you to show him every house in Kansas
City that has a for-sale sign in the front lawn."

"That's just about the size of it." She closed a drawer
in Zack's bureau and opened one of Anna's, taking the
clothes out of Seth's hands.

"Maybe he's infatuated with you, not the house, and
he'll just keep looking till you give him a date."

"Please don't threaten me like that."

A shuffling sound in the hallway announced the approach
of one of the twins. "I think they've discovered we abandoned them," Seth said.

"That will be Anna," Nikki said. "Zack never comes in
here on his own—he's afraid someone will think he actually wants to take a nap."

Anna peeked around the corner, grinned, and scrambled
across the room on hands and knees. When she reached
them, she braced her hands against Nikki's knees, hauled
herself upright, and began to babble.

"What is it, sweetheart?" Nikki asked. She bent to pick
up the baby.

"Watch out," Seth warned. "She'll drool all over you." He reached to take Anna out of her arms.

The baby held out one arm to him, but kept her other clamped around Nikki's neck. Nikki gasped as the baby pulled. "She's incredibly strong!"

"She does the equivalent of pushups about twelve hours a day," Seth pointed out. "Let go, you little octopus." His fingers brushed against Nikki's throat as he tried to peel Anna's hand loose. "I'm afraid I'll scratch you if I pull," he said.

But Anna had found a new game, and she was determined not to let go. With one arm around each neck, she tugged.

Nikki glanced at the obstinate little face so close to her own and gave in. "All right, you can have your group hug, Anna, and then you're getting down because I have to leave." Playing along, she took a step closer and laid her free hand on the back of Seth's neck, over Anna's tiny one.

Anna gave an infectious little giggle that made Nikki smile. "It takes so little to keep her happy." Nikki looked up at Seth, expecting that he, too, would be sharing the joke.

But his eyes were dark, without a spark of laughter.

She was so close she could almost drown in the emerald depths. The last lingering hint of his aftershave, mixed with the fresh scent of the outdoors, tickled her nose. His neck was warm under her hand—almost hot compared to Anna's tiny hand, cool from her crawl across the floor. Against the pad of her thumb she felt the uneven thump of his heartbeat—or was that her own?

Nikki pulled back, uncertain. "It was a joke, Seth." Her voice cracked.

"Yeah." He cleared his throat. "No news about the ship today, I suppose?"

At least they were off a touchy subject—even if the new one he'd chosen made it very clear that he was anxious to have this whole thing over with.

No more anxious than I am, Nikki thought. No wonder all his girlfriends had a certain dimness in common—they might not even notice how skittish he was.

Nikki shook her head, peeled Anna loose, and handed her over. "Not a thing. Wouldn't you think by now they could get some official guess about how long it's going to be?"

"You're getting tired of passing babies back and forth like cards in a game of war." He nestled Anna close.

Nikki tried to ignore the baby's stuck-out lower lip and her pleadingly outstretched hand. She turned back to the bureau, tucking tiny socks and undershirts into the drawers. "Well—yes. Aren't you?"

"I don't know." His voice seemed to be back to normal. "I actually found myself missing Zack today. He seems to have a talent for setting my most troublesome customer on edge."

Nikki shot him a startled look. "And that's a *good* thing?"

"If he'd been with me today, she might not have decided to move another wall and enlarge her closet to include ten feet of cabinets for her shoes."

"Emily Cooper."

"The one and only."

Nikki said, trying to sound fair, "I suppose the good thing about her is that she provides job security for all your workers."

"Yeah. If you'd like to take Zack with you tonight—"

Nikki shuddered at the thought. A child who could cause havoc on a construction site would be deadly in the sort of house she'd be showing to Neil Hamilton tonight. "It's so sweet of you to share him, Seth. But no, thanks."

Seth shrugged. "It's up to you. But I'll just about guarantee the tycoon will cut the evening short if you do."

Nikki didn't wait around to see what his next offer would be. Packing up both babies and coming along to keep her company, no doubt. And wouldn't Neil Hamilton enjoy *that* treat!

The parking area outside her townhouse was full, so Nikki had to leave her car almost a block away. As she hurried down the sidewalk toward her unit, her mind was already on the contents of her closet, so it took her longer than it normally would have to notice the two men standing outside her front door—and longer yet to realize that there was something very strange about the way they were behaving.

She slowed her step and frowned, watching, as she approached. The lightbulb above the door had burned out— or been turned off, suggested a suspicious voice in the back of her mind—and the way one of them was crouched over the doorknob set off alarm bells in her head. But just as she'd decided to veer off toward the closest neighbor's door and ask for help, one of the men turned round and saw her.

It was the manager of the complex, she saw, and relief registered in his face and Nikki's brain at the same instant.

"What's the problem?" she called as she hurried toward him.

The other man wheeled around, obviously startled. "Nikki! You're all right!"

"Richard?" She was just as surprised as he obviously was. "Of course I'm all right. What are you doing here?"

"You were going to call me," he reminded.

"Oh." She bit her lip, remembering the day at the bank when he'd offered to take her to lunch and she'd said she'd call him later in the week. "I've been a little busy, and I forgot."

"Well, you seem to have forgotten to go to work, too," he said. "I've called a half-dozen times. You haven't been there, and your receptionist has seemed very edgy about telling me anything."

After the discussion they'd had over Nikki's supposed headache, she wasn't surprised if Jen had stopped manufacturing excuses.

"For that matter," he went on, "you haven't answered your phone, either. I've been leaving messages here all week."

"My cell phone—"

"It kicks over to a message that just says you're unavailable."

Nikki pulled it out of her pocket. The screen wasn't blank, but it was dimmer than usual. "I must have forgotten to recharge it today."

"Anyway, I stopped by to ask the manager about you, and he noticed you haven't picked up your mail, either."

"And there's a bag from the dry-cleaning service in my office," the manager added. "It's been there since Monday afternoon."

"So we came down here with the master key—"

"Expecting to find me drowned in the bathtub? Honestly, Richard." Nikki bit her lip. Obviously he'd been worried—and she had to admit he'd had reason. She'd completely forgotten that blithe half-promise. But she'd said she'd call him later in the week—and that had been only a couple of days ago.

Which, she supposed, was part of the problem. Richard seemed to be taking their friendship a great deal more seriously than she was.

"I'm sorry," she said. "Look, I've been really busy, and—"

"Too busy to come home?"

The manager said hastily, "Well, now that we know you're all right, Ms. Marshall, I'll be on my way."

Richard took a deep breath. "Nikki, is there somebody else?" His voice was somber.

Nikki was stunned. *Somebody else?*

"Richard, we've had—what? Three or four dates? It's not like we're engaged!"

"No," he said. "No, it's not. I'll see you around sometime." He walked away before she could say another word.

Nikki rolled her eyes. There was one more thing for her to-do list next week—or whenever Laura got home. Take Richard out for coffee, tell him what had been going on all week, and make sure he understood that having dinner together a few times didn't mean she was serious about him, or was ever likely to be.

After the way Thorpe had trampled on her pride, she wasn't anxious to go further than the occasional evening out, no matter who her companion was. Maybe that was why she'd made her spur-of-the-moment offer of friendship to Seth, she mused—because even though she hadn't stopped to think about it, she'd known that if any guy would understand the concept of a strings-free relationship, it would be Seth Baxter.

Well, she didn't have time to think about it now. She was already running a few minutes late in picking up her client.

Neil Hamilton was nowhere to be seen when she pulled up in front of his hotel, so she parked off to the side and checked her cell phone while she waited. The battery charge was a little stronger now, but it had been plugged in for only a few minutes while she packed, and the car charger was so slow that it would take all night to recycle the battery completely.

"And I thought I was doing so well this afternoon, checking everything off my list," she muttered.

She saw Neil coming out of the hotel and let the car idle up to the entrance. A bellboy opened the door for him and he slid in beside her. Nikki let a limo go by before she ducked between a cab and a private car and out into the street. She nodded toward a brightly colored catalog which lay on the console between them. "I brought you the new multiple-listings guide," she said. "Have you looked at the books I left with you?"

"I've been very busy."

Nikki smothered a sigh. So much for hoping that Neil might take a little personal responsibility for finding a house he liked. "Perhaps you'd like to take them back to Detroit with you. Then you can let me know if you see anything you particularly want to see."

He didn't answer. "What are we looking at tonight?"

"I've got four possibilities. It's harder to convince people to let viewers come through in the evenings when they're normally home."

"If they really wanted to sell, they would."

Nikki bit her tongue. "Have you thought more about the questions I asked at first? How you'll want to use the house, how often you'll have guests? You told me you were divorced, but will it just be you living here?"

He leaned back in his seat and looked her over. "If you mean do I have a live-in girlfriend, no." His voice was silky. "So there's an opening for the position."

"If I find anybody suitable, I'll let you know." Nikki kept her tone steady. "I was thinking more about children. You know—joint custody, summer visits, holidays."

"Oh. No. Never had any of those. My ex-wife was too focused on her career. She was—is—a lawyer."

"That's interesting."

"She always seemed to think so. Personally I prefer a woman who doesn't put her home second to her career."

No wonder she didn't want to have kids with a husband whose attitude is purely medieval.

"You know," Neil mused, "real estate is such a perfect career for a woman."

Nikki said, a bit curtly, "Women have certain advantages in the field, that's true."

"No, I meant that selling houses leaves lots of time for a woman to have a family."

I should take you home with me so you can tell Seth that one—he'd get a good laugh out of the idea of me having time on my hands.

Fortunately they'd reached the first house on her list, so Nikki didn't have to answer. She consulted her notes instead. "This one is a little smaller than you wanted," she said. "There are three bedrooms, but no home office. One of the bedrooms could be converted, of course."

"But that would leave me short."

Good. You can subtract. That must be handy.

Neil walked in, looked around, shrugged, and walked out. At least, Nikki thought grimly, it looked as if the evening would be fast-paced—even without Zack to help it along. She wondered how Seth was doing with both babies. Funny that tonight he hadn't objected to being left alone with them for bath and bedtime, because he'd been so reluctant to take over the job by himself that first night. But this evening he'd seemed almost eager to shoo her out of the house.

Not that it took Einstein to figure that out. After Anna's little prank where she'd pulled them into an embrace, practically within kissing distance, no wonder he was eager for a little time on his own—even if it included two babies.

They were at the fourth house when Neil said suddenly, "That first place we looked at tonight. Why did you show it to me, when it's too small?"

Nikki held on to her patience. "Because it could be enlarged. It's a big lot, so there would be plenty of room to build on a nice-sized office."

"Oh."

She wondered how anyone with so little imagination could have possibly reached the management level. But perhaps if he only dealt with numbers, not with people or designs...

Impulsively she said, "Let me show you something. It's not an office, it's a ground-level master bedroom. But it will help you get an idea of how it can be done, to put a new wing on a house without making it look like a cancerous growth." She turned the car toward Rockhurst. "This is private property, so we can't go walking through—especially at this hour of the night. But I'll drive around the block because you can get a pretty good view from the street."

It didn't take long, in the light evening traffic, to drive from the exclusive neighborhoods she'd been concentrating on, through the shopping district at County Club Plaza, past the art museum and into the winding, narrower streets of Rockhurst.

"It's right up ahead," she said, pointing. "That big Mediterranean style house with the pink tile roof. The new wing is around back, but since the house is on a corner—"

Neil apparently wasn't listening. He had leaned forward and was staring at Emily Cooper's house.

Nikki circled the block, driving slowly, watching Neil as well as taking a look at the addition herself. It had changed an amazing amount in the two days since she'd walked through; the roof tile was in place, and—was that a new skylight?

She took a second look at Neil. He was hardly blinking, because he was staring so hard.

"That's the one," he said. "That's the house I want to buy."

CHAPTER SEVEN

No MATTER how hard Nikki tried to explain that Emily Cooper's house was not for sale, that she had only driven him past it to help him see what might be done to improve some other house, there was no budging Neil Hamilton.

He'd said once that he would know the right house when he saw it. Nikki had thought the comment had risen out of his inability to visualize and put into words exactly what it was he wanted, because it was the same kind of helpless statement she heard from clients at least once a week.

But never before had one been so stubborn about it, or so unreasonable. Never before had one fallen in love at first sight and been ready to sign a contract without even setting foot inside the front door.

As far as Neil was concerned, now that he'd seen the house he wanted, the only question left was what Nikki was going to do about it.

Which brought her right back to the beginning—trying to explain that she couldn't sell him a house which wasn't for sale.

He got out of her car in front of his hotel, then leaned back inside. "Everything's for sale," he announced. "I'll be back in town on Sunday, and I'll expect you to have some answers."

When Nikki came down the street, Laura's house was dark except for a weird flicker beyond the living room windows. For an instant she thought of fire, but the glow was more blue than red, and when she came inside she could hear the murmur of the television set. Seth was lying on the couch, his head propped against one arm and his feet, crossed at the ankles, on the other. He didn't move when she came in.

Poor guy, she thought. The babies must have worn him out. She knew the feeling well.

She stood there for an instant, just watching him—intrigued because she'd never seen him so far off guard before. Even though he seemed to have given up the habit of surveying her like a rabbit captivated by a cobra, he'd never stopped being watchful, even wary. "Running even when no one's pursuing," she muttered.

He sat up. "What was that?"

"Oh, nothing. I thought you were asleep."

"I was watching the tennis match."

"Who's winning?"

"The guy on the left, I think."

"If you don't even know who's playing, or who's ahead, then why are you watching?"

"I was waiting for you to show up. It's not like you to be so quiet. Are you having trouble coming up with an excuse for being late?"

Nikki drew back, puzzled. "And exactly what's your problem? You sound like I missed curfew." She set down the duffle bag she'd brought in.

His gaze flickered. "I tried to call you, but your cell phone was dead. I was worried. After everything you've said about Neil Hamilton—"

"You thought he'd cornered me in a bedroom somewhere?"

"It's been known to happen."

"Yes, it has. That's why women who sell real estate take self-defense classes and carry tear gas canisters on their key rings." She dangled her keys under his nose.

"In that case," he said calmly, "I won't give your keys to the twins to chew."

"Give them your own. You're the one who has an extra." A bit too late, she realized that it might not have been smart to remind him of that incident. "Truly, you were worried about me?"

"The thought crossed my mind."

"That's sweet, Seth—even if you were really more worried about who you'd get to help out if I was suddenly out of the picture." She sat down on the arm of the couch. "I need a favor."

"Nikki, so help me, if you've scheduled another day out with Neil—"

"No, no. I told you he's going back to Detroit tomorrow."

"Then it's some other client?"

"Well, there are a few things I should probably check on at the office. But what I really need is for you to tell me a little about Emily Cooper."

"Why do you want to know?"

She told him about Neil's sudden fixation with Emily's house, and when she was finished, Seth looked at her for half a minute and shook his head in disbelief. "You took him past Emily's."

"Only to give him an example of how a house can be enlarged in a way that enhances the original architecture instead of overwhelming it."

"Thank you," Seth said quietly.

"Oh. You're welcome. You do good work. I never would have shown it to him, of course, if I'd had any idea that he'd take one look at the house and fall in love with it."

"It's not the usual reaction, no."

"Exactly. How could I have anticipated that? Nobody buys a house without looking inside."

"You were telling me about someone in Mission Hills who did," Seth reminded.

"That was different. That guy never had any intention of living in it."

"So what are you going to do about Neil's obsession?"

"Well, first I need to call Emily and find out whether she'd consider selling."

"Get real, Nikki. The woman's building on a wing. She isn't thinking about moving."

"I can at least ask," Nikki said stubbornly. "If she'll just let me show him through, I'm sure he'll get over it. He's in love with an illusion, and until that's knocked out of his head, he won't even be able to see anything else."

"Emily's house?" Seth said doubtfully. "An illusion?"

"Honestly, Seth, the place looked like a magazine cover tonight, beautifully landscaped and lit. But once he gets inside and realizes that the rooms are small and cramped…"

"They're not, dear."

"Or that the bathrooms are old-fashioned…"

"That's why she's building a new one."

"Or that the kitchen isn't big enough for a caterer to work in…"

"It's huge, Nikki."

"All right," she snapped. "There will be something he doesn't like. I'll find it if I have to crawl through the attic and the basement myself. Once he sees that house for what it really is, he'll get over the whole idea and be more realistic about buying something else."

"But if Emily's not interested in selling, she's certainly not going to let you show buyers through."

Nikki bit her lip, and then quoted Neil. "Everything's for sale."

"At the right price. The question is whether he's willing to pay it. Anyway, I'm not so sure I want her to sell the place."

Nikki was startled. "Why on earth not? All week you've been talking as if your biggest goal right now is to get rid of her as a client."

"If she sells before the addition's completed, I'll probably be stuck with Neil Hamilton—and from what you've said about him, I don't think I'd like him any better."

"I may have exaggerated him a bit," Nikki said carefully. "I mean, I'm sure Emily can't really be as kooky as you've painted her, either."

"Think again, sweetheart. Besides, if Emily sells her house, she'll want me to build her a new one."

Nikki shrugged. "But before she makes up her mind what she wants, you'll be retired and off the hook."

"I'll sleep on it, Nikki." He stretched out on the couch once more, his stocking-clad feet nudging her off her perch. "See you in the morning."

Nikki looked down at him. "You don't fit on that couch very well."

"Give the girl a prize."

"How have you managed to get any sleep at all? Why haven't you said something?"

"Complaining wouldn't have accomplished anything."

"Yes, it would. I'll be right back."

"What are you going to do?"

"Sleep on the couch so you can have the bed," she said over her shoulder. "Besides, I have this terrible compulsion to watch grainy old black and white movies tonight, and there's no television set in the bedroom."

She changed into her sweats, dug out an extra blanket,

and peeked in on the babies before going back to the living room. Seth had gone into the kitchen, and she heard the refrigerator door closing as she bustled around to make her bed. She'd tucked herself in with the remote control in hand when he returned with a dish of ice cream.

"You must have felt cheated this morning at the mall," Nikki said, nodding at the bowl.

He waved his spoon at the couch. "You're sure you want to do this?"

"It's done. Go get a good night's sleep for a change."

He didn't answer, but he padded off quietly toward the master bedroom.

Nikki yawned and turned the sound down on the television. The couch wasn't the most comfortable she'd ever slept on, but at least she fit between the arms. She was surprised Seth hadn't just rolled off onto the floor where at least he could stretch out. But the cushions were delightfully warm where he'd been lying, and with the padding provided by the extra blanket, she figured she probably wouldn't have any trouble dozing off...

When she woke, she was dazed for a moment. Had she dreamed that offer to spend the night on the couch?

Because she wasn't there any more. She was in the master bedroom, tucked under the comforter. And beside her, stretched out on his side facing her—his eyes closed, his breathing peaceful—was Seth.

Before she could even think about moving slowly or carefully, Nikki had shot to a sitting position. The rocking motion of the mattress woke Seth. He opened his eyes, but moved only far enough to punch his pillow up into a wad to prop his head a little higher.

Obviously Nikki thought spitefully, he wasn't surprised at finding himself in bed with a female...

"I don't know what happened," she said. "I don't remember getting up in the night, but I must have been so out of it that I forgot I was sleeping on the couch.''

He nodded thoughtfully. The gesture looked a bit weird, considering that he was still lying down, and she thought she saw the glimmer of a smile in his eyes.

''Dammit, Seth, I certainly didn't do it on purpose,'' she snapped. ''Why would I want to get in bed with you?''

''Is that a rhetorical question or would you like a list?''

''Your ego is certainly wide awake this morning.''

''Oh, the rest of me is, too. If you'd like a demonstration…''

She slid as far toward the edge of the bed as she could.

''Come on, Nikki. I couldn't shake the idea that it wasn't very gentlemanly of me to let you sleep on the couch, so I brought you in here. You're no harder to put to bed than the babies are. A little heavier, but you sleep just as soundly.''

Nikki bristled. ''And then you stayed.''

''Well, I didn't say I was a *perfect* gentleman. It just seemed silly for either of us to be uncomfortable when there was plenty of room here.'' He sat up a little higher, and the comforter slid down off his chest.

His bare chest, Nikki noted.

He yawned. ''So, now that we have all that settled, can we grab ten more minutes of shut-eye before the twins wake up and start crowing like chickens?''

Nikki opened her mouth to protest and then realized how silly she was being. If they'd spent the night in the same bed, another few minutes certainly wasn't going to damage her virtue. That had obviously never been in question, anyway, for he was looking amused at the very idea.

They were partners, that was all, stuck in a mad adventure. If he'd had any thought that she might take their sleeping together in a romantic sense, Seth would have fled the country rather than ask for trouble by picking her up and shifting her into bed.

So she'd better get herself under control before he started questioning why she thought it was such a big deal.

She slid tentatively back down under the comforter. She almost—*almost*—wished that she hadn't been asleep when he moved her. She was neither tall nor heavy, but her experience with the twins had told her that a sleeping body seemed to be twice its actual weight. It would have been interesting to see how Seth had done it....

But then he no doubt got lots of practice with slinging things around. Not only on the construction site, but in his own bedroom. Nikki thought, a bit maliciously, that a tall blonde—even one who was the perfect size for a model— would outweigh her any day of the week...

"That's my girl," Seth said, sounding sleepy.

She almost pointed out that he'd said he was wide awake. Then she stopped to think where that might lead, and decided there was absolutely no sense in asking for trouble.

Seth draped an arm across her. Nikki tensed, and then forced each muscle to relax.

Partners, she told herself. *It's no big deal.*

The twins were unusually bright-eyed and cheerful, and far more interested in playing hands-and-knees tag than in cereal. When Nikki tried to capture them, they scrambled gleefully off in opposite directions. "I had to go and teach them that little evasion trick," she said glumly.

"Oh, let them dust the floor a bit longer," Seth said. "Go get some clothes on and we'll skip the routine today and go out for breakfast."

She surveyed the twins, who were still in sleepers, and Seth, who was sporting a stubble. "By the time we get everybody ready, it'll be more like brunch."

"That's okay. There will be less of a crowd."

"All right," she said. "But no ice cream."

"Hear that, guys? How about french toast and sausage?" Anna giggled. Zack nodded.

"They don't know what you're talking about," Nikki pointed out.

"Then it's time they learned."

The coffee shop that Seth chose was obviously used to hosting families, for there was a line of high chairs, and the twins' milk was delivered to the table in tip-proof cups. "I see you come in here a lot," Nikki said as she put bibs on the babies.

"How do you know that?"

"Because the hostess could barely stop her eyes from popping out at the sight of you with a woman and a couple of kids. Which says she's used to seeing you, but on your own." She added thoughtfully, "Or perhaps with a succession of different women... No, the sort you date would be much more likely to hold out for lunch at Felicity's."

"Ah, you're a real-estate person *and* a private detective. It's a flexible combination, I'll say that for you."

"At any rate, it's painfully obvious that the hostess had never thought of you as a family man, until this morning." *Real-estate person... Oh, yes.* "You said we'd talk about Emily Cooper today."

Seth eyed her over his coffee cup. "No, I said I'd sleep on it."

"And now that you've slept on it, what have you decided?"

"That calling her up to ask if her house is for sale will get you exactly nowhere."

"Give me credit for a little tact, Seth. I'll be diplomatic about it. But if you're not going to help me, at least promise that you won't sabotage the deal."

"I never said I wouldn't help you. But handling Emily Cooper requires a certain sideways approach."

"All right," Nikki said slowly. She took Zack's tippy cup out of his hand and turned it right side up. "I'm listening."

"No, you're not. Whenever you have the babies settled to your satisfaction, I'll tell you."

"They do require a certain amount of attention to keep them quiet, Seth."

He shook his head. "They'll occupy themselves by flirting with every customer in the whole coffee shop if you just leave them to it."

She sighed and sat back in her chair. "All right, I'm really listening."

Seth sipped his coffee and told her his plan.

Nikki stared at him for a long moment. The waitress brought their meals, and she absently cut a piece of french toast and a sausage patty into tiny bits and set it in front of the twins. "And you seriously think that will work?"

"It can't fail any more spectacularly than if you call her up from the office with the direct approach."

That much was probably true, Nikki admitted. Cold-calling a client she'd never even met was about the least promising idea she'd ever come up with. She wouldn't have considered it if Neil Hamilton hadn't been so insistent. But this scheme of Seth's wasn't a whole lot better than phoning out of the blue. "I need to stop by the office before we go," she announced. "I want to have a listing contract in my pocket, just in case."

"So you can get her signature before she changes her mind? Nikki, it'll either work or it won't."

"And if it does, I want to be ready to capitalize on it," Nikki said stubbornly.

"Fine with me. More coffee?"

The real-estate office wasn't exactly bustling—not an unusual sight for late on Thursday morning, when the agents who were working were mostly out with clients. Nikki was glad to see the almost-empty parking lot, however, because she hadn't exactly dressed the part this morning. Bryan, for instance, would never let her forget it if he saw her coming in to the office in jeans and a sweatshirt blazoned with the name of the college she'd attended. But then, she hadn't intended to come to work this morning—particularly not with Seth and the twins in tow.

She opened the door of the SUV before it had quite stopped moving. "I'll just run inside and grab that form. I'll be right back."

"And we'll just come with you," Seth said pleasantly, "in case someone tries to handcuff you to your chair to finish up whatever's pending."

"Suit yourself. You must like lifting weights better than I do, to haul the twins around any more than you need to." She hurried ahead into the office.

Jen was at her regular spot just inside the front door, talking to a man who was standing just in front of the desk. A woman beside him had leaned over the desk, apparently to write a note. Jen looked up. "Oh, Ms. Marshall—there's another counteroffer on the MacIntyre deal. I was going to call you in a little bit, but since you're here—"

"I'll take a look at it."

The two by the desk turned as Nikki spoke. It was the young couple who had just completed the purchase of their new house on Monday, in the speediest closing Nikki could remember pushing through. She felt guilty just thinking about it—even though nothing important had been skipped over, or even skimped, in the process, such a big moment deserved more time and solemnity.

The woman stepped forward with a big smile. "How

wonderful! You're here today after all. Jen thought you wouldn't be, so I was just writing you a note.''

The young man held out a package and said, ''This is just a little thank you for all you've done for us.''

Nikki felt even guiltier as she took the small, exquisitely wrapped box.

''And we'd still like you to have dinner with us,'' the young woman said. ''Just you, I mean—not a party or anything—so whenever you're free, let us know.''

The door opened behind her.

''To be perfectly honest, though, it's not just dinner,'' the man went on. ''There are a couple of things we'd like your advice about—things we're thinking of doing to the house. Some remodeling stuff.''

Seth came up beside her, and automatically Nikki reached for the nearest baby. It happened to be Zack, who twisted around in her arms and grabbed with both hands for the gold bow atop Nikki's package.

Anna squeaked a protest and went after it herself.

''Cut it out, guys,'' Seth said.

Nikki peeled Zack's fingers off the bow, with difficulty, and set the box on the corner of Jen's desk. ''That's downright embarrassing. They haven't even had a birthday yet, and they were too young last Christmas for packages to make much of an impression.''

''Maybe the fondness for wrapping paper and bows is genetic,'' the young woman said with a grin. ''I didn't realize you were married, Nikki. I thought…'' Her gaze slid to Seth. ''Oh, well.''

Nikki wondered if the client was remembering the attention Richard had paid to Nikki at the closing. Inviting her to a tête-á-tête lunch at the newest bistro on the Plaza…

''Please do bring your husband, too,'' the young woman

went on firmly. "I'd have invited you both, of course, if I'd known."

Seth held out a hand to her. "Seth Baxter," he said.

"*Not* my husband," Nikki said firmly.

"Oh." The woman's smile faded just a bit and she looked a little confused.

Nikki felt like slapping herself in the forehead. "No—no, I mean, we're not... I mean, we're just friends. And these aren't our babies. They're just borrowed."

Seth, she saw, was biting back a grin. But he sounded serious as he stepped into the breach. "Did I hear you say something about remodeling? Because I'm a contractor, and I'd be happy to give you my advice."

"Then you're exactly the person we need," the young woman said. "And that certainly explains how Nikki knows so much about the practical things around a house."

Nikki's jaw dropped. As if she'd gotten her knowledge of how a house was put together by some sort of osmosis, rather than by study, experience, and hard work!

"How about Saturday night?" the young man offered. "I'll put something on the grill and we can look the place over."

Nikki opened her mouth to object, but the date was made before she could argue. The young couple bustled out and Nikki rolled her eyes, handed Zack to Seth, took the folder Jen held out, and started toward her own little cubicle. Seth followed.

"*You're exactly the person we need,*" she quoted as she sat down behind her desk. "Great. You can go, and I'll stay home."

"You're just offended that they think I know more about how houses are put together. Which I do."

"Well, yes, you do, but that doesn't mean..." Nikki gave it up as an impossible argument.

"You don't like them?" Seth asked. "I thought they were very nice."

"They're delightful people, and I fully intended to go and visit—sometime that I don't have two babies to deal with."

"You told me Laura keeps a list of teenage baby-sitters on the refrigerator." Seth sat down across the desk from her. "Surely one of them will be free on Saturday night. And the babies need a break from us as much as we need one from them."

"I don't care to contemplate the idea that we might still have them on Saturday night. Would you just be quiet for two minutes while I read this?"

"Besides," Seth went on, "if you're going to cost me Emily Cooper's job, then I need to be out shaking the bushes for business."

"Right," Nikki sighed. "I'm really worried for you."

Seth didn't say anything, and finally she looked up at him warily. He wasn't doing anything suspicious, just sitting there in a straight chair with a twin cuddled in each arm. The late morning sunlight streaming though the window behind her desk reflected off all three heads.

He looked like a saint, complete with halo.

I'm losing it, Nikki thought, and buried herself in her paperwork.

Nikki watched as Seth unfolded the stroller in Emily Cooper's driveway and said, "This plan of yours isn't going to work."

"It certainly won't if you go into it with that attitude. Grab a kid and let's get started."

"It's not ethical."

"I told you, you have to come at Emily sideways or you'll never accomplish anything. Come on."

Nikki bit her lip. She had her choice, of course; she could either adopt Seth's plan or go it alone. Which was actually no choice at all.

A couple of minutes later they were walking around the corner of Emily's house toward the new addition, pushing the stroller and pausing now and then so Seth could point out features of the new section.

The rest of the windows had gone into place since Nikki's last visit, and the last rows of tiles were going up on the roof. Inside the new rooms, craftsmen bustled around installing cabinets, and a truck had backed up as close as possible to the glass doors so workmen could unload rolls of carpet.

"It's made a lot of progress in just a few days," Nikki said.

"Hey, remember you're not supposed to have seen it before. Hello, Mrs. Cooper. There's someone I'd like you to meet."

Emily Cooper didn't seem to hear him. "Is the work going to be finished by the weekend?"

"Not completely. But enough for the purpose."

"It had better be. So this is the young woman who's been costing me my contractor lately."

"Not exactly," Nikki said. "That would be the young woman who's riding in the stroller—"

Seth took her arm—and pinched it. Nikki shut up.

"This is my friend Nikki," he said. "She's thinking about building on a nursery and play room—as you can see, the babies could put it to good use—and I wanted to show her some of the innovative ideas that you'd come up with here."

Nikki had to give him credit. He hadn't actually told a single fib—even if it was Laura's house she was thinking about, not her own.

Emily Cooper sounded flattered. "Oh, certainly. Look around."

"Perhaps you'd like to show her through? I'll take the stroller, Nikki, so you can concentrate."

As Emily gave Nikki the grand tour, Seth followed behind, pointing out things now and then himself.

"It's such beautiful work," Nikki said. "It's a truly gorgeous house, Mrs. Cooper. Is the rest all Mediterranean inside?"

Emily Cooper preened herself. "Yes. Entirely original, I believe."

"You know, I think this house probably has everything I'm looking for," Nikki said earnestly. "I don't suppose you'd be interested…oh, no, of course you wouldn't. Anyone who had a place like this…"

"Interested in what?"

"In selling it." Nikki couldn't quite keep herself from holding her breath while she waited. But surely if her interest had actually been personal, she'd have done the same thing.

Emily Cooper stared at her, looking down the very considerable length of her nose. "Well, one can never say for certain. But I very much doubt it. However, I suppose if you'd like to bring your husband by so he could take a look… There's no sense in even talking about it unless he's interested as well."

"Actually I'm not married." Nikki saw Emily's eyes narrow in disapproval. *Obviously being a single mother isn't the right answer.* "I'm not married just now, I mean. I—" *Get yourself out of this one without telling a lie, Marshall.*

"I see," Emily Cooper said. "Now if you'll excuse my contractor for a moment, dear, there's something I need to talk to him about."

Well, that had gone precisely nowhere, Nikki reflected. She turned the stroller around with difficulty. Emily Cooper's new bedroom might be huge, but it was so crowded with workmen and tools and materials that it was hard to maneuver through the bedlam.

The stroller felt as heavy as an eighteen-wheeler as she pushed it out toward the SUV. Now that she knew a little more about Emily Cooper, however, it was clear to Nikki that Seth had been right—a direct appeal would have worked no better. At least she was no worse off for having trusted him and tried his method.

She parked the stroller in the lawn next to the SUV and leaned against a carved stone pillar by the drive. She would wait till Seth came back to put the twins in the car—in case he'd managed to pull some magic trick that would make Emily Cooper want to talk to her. But it was no more than a feeble hope which made her delay.

She was thinking about what she was going to tell Neil Hamilton when he came back to Kansas City on Sunday when she heard Seth's cheerful whistle coming around the corner of the house. Nikki felt like growling.

"Hey, champ," Seth said. "Knock off the grass-chewing, or Nikki will think you've been eating spinach again and she'll start feeding it to you every day."

She spun around to face the stroller. Zack had leaned as far as he could from his seat, pulled up a handful of grass, and started chomping on it almost as efficiently as a pony would. "Oh, no. Why are you grinning? You mean he's done this before?"

"And it hasn't seemed to hurt him a bit," Seth said. "But that's not why I'm grinning. Guess what Emily wanted to talk about."

"How should I know? She wants to move another wall, I suppose."

"Nope. She wanted to warn me about you. She thinks you're not on the up-and-up."

"You mean she saw through your little scheme?"

"Oh, no. She pulled me aside to say that she doubts you were ever married at all."

"Imagine that," Nikki said feebly.

Seth grinned. "Worse yet, she thinks you're out to snag me. Quite a romantic, our Emily. Come on, let's get the kids in the car."

"So what's next?"

"Next," he said, "is a stop at my office to look at the plans of the house."

Nikki's eyes widened. "You have floor plans of this house?"

"Only rough ones, to get ready for the addition. But it's something."

"Seth, if I can just borrow the plans, Neil wouldn't have to look at the house!"

"You actually think Neil Hamilton can look at a blueprint and visualize the finished product?"

Nikki sighed. "No. He can't even look at a finished product and imagine it with different carpet and drapes."

"Then there's no point in confusing him with the drawings—but you can look at them."

"So then I can tell him about the house? I don't know how effective that will be, but I can try. And I truly appreciate the help."

"No," he said. "So when you show him through on Sunday night, you won't mistake a closet door for a room."

Nikki wasn't sure she'd heard him right. When it finally sank in, she gave a little shriek, threw her arms around his neck, and kissed his cheek. "You talked her into letting me show it? Seth, you're wonderful!"

He staggered back a step. "Not exactly," he warned. "I

got us an invitation to Emily's housewarming party. Sunday, seven o'clock, cocktails. Bring Neil, and while we're wandering around making inane conversation, he can be looking at the house.''

"Maybe I should have told her I was married after all," Nikki mused.

"And introduced Neil as your husband? Probably just as well you didn't, Nikki. I wouldn't put it past her to be looking out the window, and if she sees this…''

"This?" Nikki realized belatedly that when she'd rushed at him, Seth had caught hold to steady her, and she was still wrapped his arms. "Oh. You mean us standing here like this.''

"Not quite," Seth said. "I'm talking about this.''

Then, with infinite gentleness, he bent his head and kissed her.

CHAPTER EIGHT

HE TASTED like coffee. Freshly brewed and very tasty coffee, with a caffeinelike jolt that went straight to Nikki's brain. But instead of sharpening her perceptions, this wallop made everything grow fuzzy. She didn't even know how long he kissed her before a wolf whistle from one of the carpet-delivery guys drew his attention, and Seth slowly raised his head and let her go.

Not long, she thought, because her blood vessels couldn't have stood the pressure.

A soft pat on her rear made Nikki jerk upright and wheel around—but it was only Anna, quietly objecting to the fact that no one was paying attention to her at the moment. The baby grinned and held up her arms, begging to be picked up.

"I probably shouldn't have done that," Seth said. He leaned over Zack and released the safety harness to take him out of the stroller.

Nikki, feeling a little shaky, steadied herself against the SUV for a moment before she lifted Anna. "Why not?" she said. She was proud of herself. Her voice was lower than usual, but it didn't crack. "It was no big deal. And if your goal is to keep Mrs. Cooper off balance, I'd say that probably did it." *It certainly has* me *off balance.*

"I must say I like having Emily worried about me," Seth mused. "As long as she thinks you're trying to snag me, as she so elegantly phrased it—"

"She's less likely to be bugging you about walls." Nikki nodded. "Right. So was that enough of a show, or do you

135

want to wait five minutes till the carpet-layer has spread the gossip through the entire construction site, and then do a second act?''

Seth paused and tipped his head to one side, contemplating. ''If you think it's a good idea, I'm willing to play along.''

No. Not a good idea at all. The very idea made her brain feel a little hazy. Of course, Nikki told herself, she should have known he'd call that bluff—just as certainly as she knew that he was bluffing right now, himself. If she challenged him, he'd just laugh. So that was exactly what she should do—dare him to kiss her again—and that would be the end of the game.

Wouldn't it? Surely he wouldn't think she wanted him to kiss her... Confused, she waited just an instant too long to speak up.

Seth put Zack into his car seat and turned back to her with a smile. ''Are you having to think about it, Nikki?'' he murmured. ''That's interesting.''

''Think about what?'' Nikki tried to sound unconcerned.

His smile widened.

She handed Anna to him and tried to fold the stroller up, with minimal success. ''How on earth does Laura manage this on her own?''

''Are you changing the subject?'' Seth asked. ''Here, I'll get it.''

But he didn't push the matter. He let it drop and talked about other things on the drive from Rockhurst to his office. Which only confirmed, Nikki told herself, that she'd been right in the first place. He'd just been amusing himself.

She'd better keep a close eye on him. As far as she knew, he'd gone four days without so much as a glimpse of a tall blond model-type—phone calls, she thought, probably didn't count. The man was going to start feeling desperate soon, and then there was no predicting what he might do.

"Penny for your thoughts," Seth said.

Nikki jumped. "Why?" Too late, she realized she sounded panicky.

"Because we've been here in the parking lot for well over a minute and you hadn't noticed yet—so whatever's occupying your mind must be far more interesting."

"Oh—no, I was just… This is where your office is?" She'd never had any reason to wonder where his business was headquartered, and the sight of the sprawling two-story warehouse startled her.

"You probably thought I operated out of a storage shed somewhere."

That was true enough. Not that she'd admit it. "I had no idea you'd need so much room."

"I probably don't, but it's central and easy to get in and out of, and we can park all the construction trailers inside at once if we need to."

"All of them?" she said blankly. "How many crews do you have working?"

"In the average week, six."

"You mentioned a kitchen in Mission Hills, but I thought—"

"That I probably couldn't handle more than a couple of jobs at a time, and that's why Emily Cooper's been frustrating me so much." It wasn't a question.

"Sorry," Nikki said.

"That reminds me, though. I haven't checked on the Mission Hills job in almost a week. I need to fit a visit in one of these days."

"Do whatever you need to. We're just along for the ride. I must say it's nice to have a chauffeur, though. Getting these two to and from the supermarket yesterday—with all the bags—was quite a trick.''

''It'll be nice when they're walking,'' Seth said as he hefted the twins out of the SUV.

''Oh, really? I already know what I'm getting Laura for their birthday.''

''Wet suits so she can just run them through the car wash after they eat?''

''No. A pair of leashes.''

''Good idea. I'll spring for the rhinestone-studded collars.''

''I wasn't talking about dog leashes, for heaven's sake.'' Nikki saw him grin and bit her tongue.

Inside the office, a gray-haired woman was running envelopes through a postage machine. Nikki was a bit surprised at the sight. If she'd expected Seth to have a secretary at all, she would have expected someone young, curvy, and gorgeous, not a woman who was definitely past middle age. But then perhaps Seth had figured out that stunning blondes made better girlfriends than employees.

''Nora's my office manager,'' Seth said.

Nora was staring at the twins. ''Either I'm seeing double, Seth, or there are two of them today.''

''Better get your eyes checked, Nora. This is Nikki. I've been teaching her some practical things this morning.'' Seth smiled at Nikki.

Nikki blinked in surprise. Surely he wasn't talking about that ridiculous kiss... She could feel her face heating up.

Then it dawned on her that he was just quoting the young couple at her office this morning. *That's how Nikki knows all the practical things about houses...* They had assumed she'd learned it from associating with Seth.

She felt like sticking her tongue out at him.

"Nora, would you dig out those rough floor plans for the Cooper house? Nikki wants to look at them."

Nora handed him a stack of messages and swivelled her chair around to a file cabinet behind her desk.

Seth paged through the notes. "There are a couple of things I need to deal with here, Nikki. It shouldn't take me long. There's a table through there to spread the plans out on. But watch out for Zack, okay? He likes to eat them." He shifted Anna over his shoulder like a bag of rice and strode off toward his office.

"I'd offer to help out," Nora said as she flipped through the files, "but the little guy doesn't seem to like me."

Indeed, Nikki could feel Zack's fingers digging into her shoulders. He might be tiny, but he was incredibly strong. He was peeking out at Nora, keeping a steady eye on her, as if he expected her to make a grab for him despite the fact that her back was turned. "So that's how Seth got the scratches on his neck."

"You thought he'd been dallying with a woman?"

Now Nikki's face really felt hot. "Of course not. I mean—it wouldn't be any of my business if he did."

Nora turned around with a sheaf of papers in her hand. She didn't comment, but she looked skeptical.

He's not irresistible, you know, Nikki wanted to say. *I've been resisting him quite efficiently.*

Except, of course, that wasn't quite true. That kiss this morning had been an eye-opener. It would be no wonder, really, if women lined up to let Seth walk on them.

She took the plans and went into the conference room.

Seth had said they weren't actually blueprints, only rough drawings of the house—so she'd expected sketches that he'd made on the site as he walked through, or perhaps something that he'd quickly drawn from memory after a visit. Instead, these were careful, analytical drawings, with every room labeled, every element in precise proportion, and every significant measurement marked. From these drawings, she could almost have rebuilt Emily Cooper's house—if she'd had the necessary construction skills.

She pulled a chair up and began to study the layout. These drawings showed only the original house, so there must be another set somewhere—perhaps on the site for the workmen's use—showing the details of the new wing he was building. The rooms were nicely sized and arranged in a pattern which allowed for pleasant traffic flow. Seth was right about the kitchen—it was huge—and there was a formal dining room and a library near the front door which would serve beautifully as an office.

In short, it had just about everything Neil Hamilton was looking for. "Damn," she said.

Zack waved his arms and complained at being held, and after a quick glance around to be sure there were nothing that could damage him, Nikki set him on the floor and turned her attention back to the plans.

She didn't hear Seth until he was standing beside her. "How are the drawings?"

"Terrible."

"Really? I thought they were pretty clear, myself." He put Anna down on the floor with Zack.

"Oh, they're clear, all right. You've got a very good draftsman."

"Thanks."

There was something about the tone of his voice which made her look at him more closely. "You did these yourself?"

"Hobby of mine. Have you found the flaw yet?"

"In the house? No," Nikki said slowly. "What have I missed?"

"Heck if I know. You told me you could find one, so Neil wouldn't want the house."

"That was the goal," Nikki said gloomily. "But judging by the peek I got this morning and the floor plan... I'm afraid he'll love it."

"I suppose you could tell him she's set some outrageous price."

"That wouldn't be ethical." She planted both elbows on the drawings and looked again, hoping to find something she'd overlooked before.

"Plus you're afraid that no matter how outrageous it was, he'd agree to pay it, and then you'd really be in the soup."

Nikki nodded. "I'll already be on thin ice if I take him to see it without telling Mrs. Cooper why." She folded up the drawings. "Thanks for letting me look. At least I know what I'm up against."

"You have till Sunday night to form a plan."

"Or to stew about it."

"So let's take your mind off it for a while. Let's see... We could go to the zoo."

"You're joking."

"Don't you think the kids are up to a stroll to look at the animals?"

"Probably—but I know darn well I'm not. It's not even lunchtime yet and I'm exhausted. I was thinking more about a nap all around." She heard a distinct sniff from the outer office, which left no doubt that Nora had put her private interpretation on that comment. Before Seth could add his own spin, Nikki went on, calmly, "Anyway, I thought you needed to go check on your job in Mission Hills."

"If you don't mind."

"I'd like to see it."

"With kids in tow? Some other day would do."

Some other day. It was casual, careless—as if there would be many other times for her to see his work.

And why not, Nikki asked herself. If they were going to be friends after all this was over, then of course she'd be recommending him to clients and maybe visiting job sites to see how things were going.

If that was a good thing, however, why did it leave her feeling just a little empty?

But she didn't have time to think about it. From the corner of her eye, she saw Zack start to pull himself up next to a stainless steel cart in the corner of the room. His little hand stretched up toward the mirror-shiny coffee urn on top of the stand, and her heart almost stopped. She'd checked the floor before she'd put him down, but it hadn't occurred to her to survey every piece of furniture in the room.

Nikki moved so fast that her chair went flying. She stepped over Anna, who was on her way to join her twin, and before Zack could touch the hot urn, she'd caught him under the arms and swooped him up, out of danger.

He giggled at the game, but looked longingly over her shoulder. "Hot," she told him. "Your fingers will hurt if you touch it."

Seth picked up her chair and set it back in place by the conference table. "Good catch. Are you finished with the plans?"

In the main room, Nora had gone back to stamping envelopes. "You know, boss," she said mildly, "if the number of kids you bring in to work with you keeps doubling every couple of days like this, we're going to be knee-deep in babies by the end of next week. Won't that be fun?"

"You can start a day-care in the back room," Seth said over his shoulder, and held the door for Nikki. "You'd really take inspecting a kitchen over going to the zoo?"

"If those are the choices, yes. Oh—can we stop in the Plaza? It's almost on the way."

"Sure. Where do you need to go?"

"The Tyler-Royale store. My bill must have been sitting in my mailbox all week, and if I don't pay it today, they'll probably put my picture on a most-wanted poster. It'll just take a minute, if you want to drop me off and drive around the block."

But despite the popularity of the open air shopping district, there was a parking place just down the street from the huge department store, directly across from the carriage-ride concession.

"Look, there are a couple of carriages out," Seth said. "I thought they only ran on weekends at this time of year."

Zack bounced in his seat, pointed at the nearest horse, and announced, "Dog!"

Seth looked at him in the rearview mirror. "I suggest you not even consider applying to veterinarian school, champ."

Nikki laughed, and Zack frowned as if his feelings were hurt. "I'm sorry, darling," she said.

"Quite all right," Seth said lightly.

"I wasn't apologizing to you," Nikki pointed out. "I'll be right back."

"Don't hurry."

He obviously meant it, for when she came back he'd carried the twins across the street to look at the horses. Nikki went to join them.

"You're out of breath," Seth said.

"I took the stairs rather than waiting for the elevator."

"Didn't want to miss this, hmm? It's not quite as electrifying as the zoo, but it'll do. How about a ride?"

Zack protested at being removed from nose-patting distance, while Anna seemed relieved to be away from the huge animal.

Nikki climbed into the old-fashioned black carriage, and Seth handed the twins up to her before getting in himself. The carriage started with a jolt and settled into a plodding pace, up and down the wide streets, lined with Spanish-style brick and tile buildings.

"You know, I don't remember ever seeing that fountain," Nikki said, pointing to a statue in a reflecting pool on the corner. "Is it new?"

Seth shook his head. "It's been here since about the time the Plaza was built. But when you drive though here, you're generally thinking about traffic, not the sights." He settled Anna more comfortably on his knee.

He was right, Nikki thought. Even as a passenger in the SUV, she'd been watching other cars, looking for a parking place, and keeping an eye on the intersections which relied on politeness rather than stop signs for traffic control. The architecture had been only a faint background, and she'd paid no attention at all to things like the bright tile patterns laid into sidewalks and walls. And when she was behind the wheel herself, she usually noticed even less.

"Sometimes I've been irritated at the carriages for holding things up," she admitted.

Seth smiled at her. "There's nothing wrong with slowing the pace a little now and then."

With a half-conscious sigh, she settled back into the corner of the carriage to enjoy the ride. It was a beautiful Indian-summer day, warm and sunny, and the slow movement of the carriage created just a slight cooling breeze. The clop-clop of hooves was almost hypnotic, and the carriage swayed a little from side to side as the horse followed his prescribed route, paying no attention to the cars which swung around the carriage and sped on.

Zack waved both arms energetically and said, "Damn!"

Nikki stared at the baby in shock. "Did he just say what I think I heard? I've been talking to him all week—how could he possibly pick out the one word that he's not supposed to repeat?"

"Maybe because you saying it reinforced the fact that he heard it while I was working on the dishwasher."

"But the child's entire vocabulary consists of six words."

"Really? He talks that much?"

"So why does the one that comes out sounding clear have to be the one…"

"Give it up, Nikki. The more you try to stop it, the more delighted he'll be to show off."

She sighed and relaxed again.

People on the sidewalk noticed the twins, and Zack, seeing them point, happily waved bye-bye. "You're a little ham," Nikki accused. She looked over his head at the crowd, blinked, and looked again. Could it be?

"What's the matter?" Seth said.

She'd been right. Richard was just coming out of the popular new bistro that he'd offered to take her to, accompanied by a man in a dark suit—probably a fellow banker. She turned her head away and sat Zack up a little higher on her lap. "Nothing. I just saw someone I know."

Seth cast an eye over the crowd. "You mean Richard Houston?"

She was startled. "You know him, too?"

"Sure. Contractors spend almost as much time at the bank as real-estate people do. If I'm not borrowing money to start a job, I'm helping my customer get a home-equity loan to pay for it."

"I hadn't thought of that."

"So why are you dodging Richard? Do you owe him money, too?" His tone was lazy.

"I'm not dodging him."

Seth's eyes narrowed. "It certainly looks like it. You're using Zack like a shield. What's the matter, Nikki?"

"Nothing, really. I'd just as soon not have Richard asking questions right now."

"Why? You're surely not ashamed to tell him why you've got possession of two babies."

"Of course not. Just—"

"I see. He's the banker you're dating."

The banker I used to be dating, she almost said. But she stopped herself in time. She wasn't about to try explaining that Richard was annoyed at her for not returning his calls and she was annoyed at him for seeming to think he had a proprietary right to know where she was at all times. She wasn't sure yet exactly how much she was going to tell Richard. But one thing was dead certain—whatever she did, it was none of Seth's concern.

But somehow, just seeing Richard—being reminded of that particular piece of unfinished business—had taken the edge off her joy in the ride.

They were well on the way home before Nikki noticed the route Seth was taking. "I thought you were going to stop in Mission Hills."

He glanced in the mirror toward the twins. "I'll do it some other time. The kids are starting to look cranky."

Nikki hadn't noticed.

"After all that fresh air," Seth went on, "it would probably be smarter to get a bit of food into them and put them down for a nap, not drag them through another construction site."

She couldn't exactly argue with that. In any case, she'd

already said once that she wanted to see his kitchen project, so it would hardly be polite to insist.

Zack went to sleep in his high chair, his face dropping onto the tray. Nikki had to brush chunks of ham and cheese off his cheek when she picked him up. Anna clung and wanted to be rocked, but in a matter of minutes she was out, too.

When Nikki tiptoed out of the twins' room, there was no sound in the house. The garage door was open, she noticed, so she stepped out onto the driveway. "Seth? Do you want some lunch?"

He came out of the garage, pushing a battered lawn-mower, a small gas can in one hand. "Maybe after I finish the lawn. It's getting a little shaggy, and who knows what it will look like by the time Steve gets home." He bent over the mower to fill the tank.

"If you'd like help—"

"Are you offering to take turns pushing?"

"Not exactly," Nikki said, tongue firmly in cheek. "I'll send Zack out when he wakes up. I'm sure he'll be happy to eat all the clippings."

There were a million things Nikki should be doing—reviewing the new listings which she'd picked up at the office that morning, phoning some clients to see if they'd finished thinking and decided to act. Instead she baked chocolate chip cookies, and when the first pan came out of the oven she clipped the baby monitor to her belt and took a tall glass of milk and a plate outside to Seth.

The mowing was mostly done, and the sharp scent of bruised grass mingled with the aroma of chocolate and but-ter as Nikki crossed the lawn to the back fence toward the roar of the mower. She circled a big lilac bush that was badly in need of pruning, and caught a glimpse of Seth.

He'd taken off his shirt and hung it on a fence post while he worked.

She'd seen him bare-chested that morning in the bedroom, when the comforter had slid down, but this was different. In the sunlight his skin gleamed gold, and his muscles rippled rhythmically as he pushed the mower back and forth.

He looked up and smiled, and Nikki's head began to spin again just as it had that morning in Emily Cooper's driveway when he'd kissed her.

How quickly, she thought, they'd grown comfortable together. Not that the sensation she was feeling at this instant was precisely comfortable, of course, for her ears were buzzing as if she was on an adrenaline high. But in the space of a few days, they'd gone from near-strangers to sharing laughter, jokes, and the duties and the joys in an easy, almost intimate way.

She was going to miss this, when it was all over and life got back to normal.

If, her conscience whispered, *it would ever be normal again.*

Nikki took a long bubble bath after the babies were tucked in for the night, and argued with herself until the water grew cold about what she should say to Seth regarding sleeping arrangements. It was a bit of a dicey subject, after all. It would be only polite to indicate—somehow—that she wasn't expecting him to spend another tortuous night on the couch. Yet she didn't exactly want to seem eager for him to join her in the bedroom, either.

And what she *really* didn't want was for the two of them to retire at the same time, like some long-married couple, to lie next to each other in the dark stillness until sleep overtook them.

Waking up next to him had been one thing. It hadn't been her idea, and by the time she realized what was going on, the episode was practically ended. But going to sleep next to him... well, that was another thing altogether. Seth would probably say she was being a prude, and perhaps she was. Still...

Seth was sitting at the dining room table with a handheld computer, poking buttons with a stylus, and he barely looked up when she came in.

"Playing solitaire?" she asked lightly. "Or doing something more exciting?"

"Figuring a bid. At least I'm doing the preliminaries so the next time I'm in the office without a twin to keep me company I can actually produce a materials list and a final price."

"It's been a long week all the way around," Nikki said. "I'm going to bed. I just wanted to say—well..."

"I won't disturb you, Nikki."

"No, that's not... I mean, we're partners, right? We need each other, and we both need our sleep. It's no big deal." She didn't wait for an answer.

It was hours later when an ear-shattering scream from the twins' room brought Nikki straight upright—but Seth was already standing beside Zack's crib when she skidded around the corner and went in.

Zack's eyes were wide and staring vacantly, and Seth looked as if he'd prefer to be anywhere except right there.

"It's okay," she said. "He has night terrors once in a while."

"Nightmares, you mean?"

"Sort of, but worse. It's more like the way a sleepwalker reacts. His eyes are open but he's not aware of anything."

"You've seen this before?"

She nodded and reached into the crib to carefully pick

up the baby. "He had one the first night I stayed here. Hand me that blanket, would you?"

Seth got a lightweight blanket from the back of the rocking chair, and Nikki swaddled Zack in it and carried him out of the room. She wasn't quick enough, however, for Anna had also awakened and started to cry.

Zack's shrieks had died to sobs, but no matter what Nikki did, he seemed to be completely inconsolable. Finally she took him into the bedroom and lay down with him on her chest, his ear against her heart, rubbing his back. The bedside clock said it was just past three in the morning.

Seth appeared in the doorway a minute later, with Anna still in his arms. She reached out for her twin.

"You might as well stretch out and be comfortable," Nikki said. "Zack's not going to settle down completely for a while, and Anna won't be happy if she can't see him."

Seth muttered something under his breath, tucked the comforter around Nikki and Zack, and lay down beside them. Anna stretched a hand out from her perch on his chest and let it rest on Zack's shoulder.

Nikki felt herself drifting off as the rhythmic motion of rubbing soothed her just as it did Zack.

The room was gray with dawn when she woke, lying on her side with Zack tucked up against her. He was starting to root around as he began to wake up. "Oh, honey," she said groggily. "Just a little longer, okay?"

Then she sniffed. The scent of coffee was drifting through the half-open bedroom door. Seth must already be up, then…

But he wasn't. He was still right there beside her, sound asleep, with Anna nestled close on his chest.

The door opened wider, and Nikki thought for an instant she was hallucinating as the last person she'd expected came into the room, carrying a tray. "Good morning, sleepyheads," Laura said cheerfully. "Are you decent?"

CHAPTER NINE

MAYBE, Nikki told herself hopefully, she was having one heck of a nightmare, and Laura wasn't actually standing there at all.

Certainly there were some telltale signs that she was locked in a dream state. For one thing, Nikki couldn't seem to move. Not a single muscle would respond to her desperate urging—even her eyelids seemed to be frozen.

For another, despite her paralysis, she seemed to be viewing the scene from two places at once—from her prone position on the bed, but also from somewhere above, looking down on the sight.

And what a sight it was. Seth flat on his back in the middle of the bed, with Anna lying on her tummy on his chest, her knees drawn up under her. Nikki on her side, with her spine nestled against Seth and Zack cradled protectively in the curve of her arm. The down comforter tucked snugly around all of them. And Laura, standing beside the bed with a tray containing two steaming cups...

Maybe I'm dead, Nikki thought, *and that's why I'm having an out-of-body experience.*

Frankly, she decided, that explanation sounded more pleasantly inviting than trying to make sense out of everything.

If she put her mind to it, Nikki supposed she could come up with a more embarrassing scenario. But at the moment, she couldn't think what it would be—and her brain didn't seem to be any more functional than her body was.

Laura took a step closer, and that was when Nikki realized that things could, indeed, get worse. Right behind Laura was Stephen, holding a video camera trained on the foursome in the bed. The lens looked the size of an observatory telescope, and the small red light which warned that the camera was taping blinked as brilliantly as a strobe, jarring Nikki's light-sensitive pupils.

I'll confess. I'll confess to anything, just turn the lights off!

"Hey, this is great," Stephen said. "This piece of tape will be a terrific hit at the wedding reception."

Nikki's heart stopped. "Wedding?" she croaked. "What are you talking about?"

Seth groaned and rolled toward Nikki. Anna started to slide off his chest, and he clapped a hand onto the baby's back and held her in place. But he didn't open his eyes. "The twins' weddings," he said. "Steve's already assembling a most-awkward-moments video to show at the rehearsal dinners. He won't admit it, but I think the plan is to threaten them with so much mortification that they'll elope instead of planning big expensive ceremonies."

Oh great. Nikki told herself. *What a dolt you are.* For a minute there, she'd actually wondered if Stephen thought their presence in the same bed was some sort of declaration of intentions. But that had been shock and embarrassment talking. Nobody in their right mind would believe there was anything romantic going on here—not with a pair of year-old babies as chaperones.

With a sort of snap, Nikki's muscles finally came back under her control. She sat up, inching away from Seth onto her own side of the bed. Her spine felt suddenly cold.

Let's start over. Act casual, she ordered herself. *Treat it as if this is no big deal—because it isn't.* "Uh—Hi, Laura. Stephen. When did you get home?" Her voice didn't seem to want to work.

"Just a few minutes ago," Laura said. "They finally brought the ship into port last night and said they would make arrangements today to get everyone back home. But we didn't want to give the health department a chance to change their minds at the last minute."

"I can understand that," Nikki said.

"So we packed as fast as we could, talked our way past the deck crew, grabbed the first cab we saw and headed for the airport." Laura smiled. "It was sort of like a spy thriller, actually—grabbing the last seats on a plane and flying halfway across the continent in the wrong direction in order to make a connecting flight. Do you have any idea how hard it is to travel across the country in the middle of the night?"

"The adventure doesn't seem to have hurt you any," Nikki said. "You look great. Rested, tanned..."

"We couldn't do anything for a whole week but lie around on deck."

"On deck?" Seth muttered. "What's the matter with you, Steve? With a handy excuse like the need to avoid infection, you didn't stay locked in the cabin for the whole week?"

Laura flashed her dimples at him. "Well, we managed to stay away from the blasted virus, if that satisfies you, Seth. Anyway, by the time we could get to a phone to tell you we were on the way, it was so late that we decided just to wait and surprise you."

Seth sat up. Anna grumbled and rooted a little closer. "Well, you managed that, all right," he said.

"Yes, I see." Laura's gaze flitted once more over the foursome in the bed. "I do hope you haven't been letting them sleep with you all week."

"Nope," Seth said lazily. "Last night was a special treat

for all of us. I'll swap you a baby for a cup of that coffee. Or did you bring it in for Anna and Zack?''

"Oh—of course." Laura set the tray between them on the comforter and reached across Nikki to pick up Anna. The baby grimaced, stretched, opened her eyes, looked straight at her mother—and started to cry.

"Sweetheart," Laura said, sounding heartbroken, "it's Mommy!"

"Remember her, Anna?" Seth said lazily. "She's the woman who abandoned you." He cradled a mug in his hand and lounged back against the pillows.

"That's not funny, Seth."

"Well, you must admit that's how it appears from her point of view. Give her back to me for a minute so she can look at you from a distance and get over the shock."

Anna's cries had awakened Zack, who blinked and looked around as if uncertain where he was. He spotted Laura, tipped his head to one side, and said sweetly, "Damn!"

Nikki put her hands over her ears.

Laura started to giggle and sat down hard on the foot of the bed, Anna still wriggling wildly in her arms. Nikki hadn't picked up her mug from the tray yet; the cup slid as the mattress bounced, and coffee surged over the rim, puddled on the tray, and began to ooze over the edge and onto the comforter. She grabbed for the mug and mopped up as much of the mess as she could with the tail of her T-shirt. Zack, dislodged by her fast movement, started to wail.

Stephen swung the camera around so he wouldn't miss an instant.

"Great moments in modern film," Seth said lazily. "Now that we've won our place in movie history, Nikki, let's get out of the way and leave these people to get reacquainted.'' He rolled out of bed without spilling a drop of his coffee, though Nikki's cup sloshed threateningly again. ''Real life is still out there waiting.''

He was gone long before Nikki had finished packing her clothes.

The interrupted night, topped off by the morning's shock and the sudden lifting of responsibility, combined to leave Nikki feeling groggy and bleary-eyed.

Real life is still out there waiting. It was true enough, but that didn't make the readjustment any easier. By the time she got to work, she still felt a bit as if she were sleepwalking.

Bryan poked his head into her cubicle. ''Is it only wishful thinking, or have you shed your little helper? Now maybe we can get some work done around here. How are you doing with Neil Hamilton?''

Nikki reached into her desk drawer for an aspirin. But she had a feeling she was going to need a whole lot more than just one before the day was over.

The MacIntyres' offer had finally gone through, and with a contract in hand signed by all parties, Nikki settled down to the paperwork of arranging a closing date. If she dropped everything off at the bank today…

It meant seeing Richard, but of course that was inevitable. Maybe it was better to get it over with right away.

She frowned, thinking about how her automatic reaction had been to avoid him. But where had that come from? She liked Richard—she just wasn't wild about this newly possessive attitude of his. A few dates didn't give them that kind of intimate claim on each other. After all, she hadn't phoned him up and asked if he'd help her out with the babies. *If we were serious about each other, it would have been a different thing entirely.*

She wondered, only half humorously, what he would say if she told him that the other man in her life—the one who had been absorbing so much time lately—was just short of a year old. That he and his sister and his uncle had become the center of her world for a few days, and now that the adventure was all over she was feeling lost and lonely. She was missing the babies...

But even more than the twins, her conscience whispered, she was missing Seth. In just a week, she had grown attached to the babies—but she had grown to love Seth.

You didn't ask Richard for help with the babies. You asked Seth instead.

Yes, he was the babies' uncle, and their godfather. But that wasn't why she'd thrown herself at him and asked for help.

The realization was like having a few dozen cymbals going off inside her head.

Nikki tried for most of the morning to argue herself out of it. This just couldn't be happening to her. She wouldn't allow it to happen. It had all been an accident—this feeling of intimacy, of important things shared—and she could not possibly have been crazy enough to fall in love with Seth Baxter.

Simply being in the same house for days on end, in such an intimate and domestic situation, was what had put the idea into her mind in the first place. Once she had her feet back on the ground in the real world, this awkward feeling would go away. The idea of falling in love with him would probably never even occur to her again—because she wasn't interested in Seth. Not really. Not in any serious way.

After this is over, maybe we can be friends, she'd told him once this week. And that was exactly what she'd meant. There had been nothing romantic about her feel-ings—because if there had been, Seth would have sensed it, skittish male that he was. He'd barely been able to keep from climbing the walls the night she'd cooked dinner for him—it was dead certain he would never have come within a mile of sharing a bed with her if he'd thought she'd take it seriously.

No. It was all her imagination, born of exhaustion and propinquity. She'd get over it.

At least, she'd better get over it, she told herself grimly. And fast. Or else he'd make sure that she would never catch a glimpse of him again.

By sheer willpower Nikki managed to finish the MacIntyres' paperwork before noon. She was on her way downtown to the bank to drop everything off when she found herself in the warehouse district and—on an impulse she couldn't explain—stopped at Seth's office.

The odds of him actually being there, she knew, were slim. She'd probably have a better chance of finding him cracking the whip over his crew at Emily Cooper's house, trying frantically to finish up the last-minute work before Sunday's housewarming party. Or he might be out in Mission Hills supervising work on the fancy new kitchen. Or any of half a dozen other places—either checking on a current job or bidding for a new one.

But she could still accomplish her purpose. She could leave a message for him with his secretary; that was the most important thing. But she could also feel out her re-action to being exposed to things which reminded her of him. She could prove to herself once and for all that this crazy sensation wasn't real. The very suspicion of being in love with him was uncomfortable, and a bit scary. But in the end, she told herself, it would turn out to be no more real than the pink elephants a drunk saw when coming off a very long bender.

Then she could go back to business as usual. She could see him at Emily's party, share birthday cake when the twins turned a year old, even swap gossip about his girlfriends with Laura—and it wouldn't bother her. But first she had to put the silliness behind her by demonstrating that it was only an odd notion born of equal parts propinquity and exhaustion.

Everything about the warehouse looked just about the same as it had yesterday, when they'd come in together, each carrying a twin. Nora was at her desk; the lights were off in the conference room; Seth's office was quiet and the door was half-closed. But despite the similarities, Nikki knew right away that Seth wasn't anywhere around. It was too calm. Yesterday there had been a sort of crackle in the air, a feeling of excitement.

Or had that crackle been inside her, because she had been with him?

"Hello, Nora," she said. "Will you give Seth a message for me?"

"That's what I'm for," the secretary said dryly. "Sometimes it seems passing along messages is the only thing I do."

Nikki wasn't about to step into the middle of the friendly squabble over Nora's duties. "The dinner we were supposed to go to tomorrow has been postponed. I'll let him know when it's rescheduled. And would you mind if I look at those drawings again? I wanted to make some notes, and I couldn't yesterday because of the baby."

Without a word, Nora pulled the file from the cabinet and handed it over. As Nikki took it into the conference room, the door of Seth's office opened wider.

Nikki was startled—not only by the movement but by

the fact that she was surprised. She had been so certain that he wasn't there—so positive that if he was in the building, she would have felt his presence.

But that's good news, she told herself firmly. She wasn't as tuned in to him as she'd been afraid she might be.

It wasn't Seth who came out of the office, however, but a thin-looking blonde in a tailored black suit. Her slim-cut slacks and high-heeled boots made her look about eight feet tall.

Nikki went on into the conference room.

The blonde said to Nora, "So that's the woman he's been playing house with." It didn't sound like a question, and the secretary didn't answer. "Well, at least he's got baby dolls out of his system."

It's just as well that I canceled that dinner, Nikki thought. She wondered if Seth would even have remembered to go.

Nikki jotted down the measurements of the major rooms in Emily Cooper's house and made a rough sketch of the main floor. Then she returned the file to Nora and tucked her notes into her briefcase.

Behind her, the office door opened. She glanced over her shoulder.

But even if she hadn't been able to see Seth beyond the plate glass, the surge of electricity in her bones would have warned Nikki who was there. She couldn't quite decide whether to be grateful for the early-warning alarm, or terrified at the confirmation that her body had turned itself into a radio antenna which received just one frequency— Seth's.

He'd only kissed her once, for heaven's sake—why on earth was she vibrating just because the man set foot within a hundred yards?

Because you've been fooling yourself. Because you were right the first time.

Because you're in love with him.

She turned around slowly.

"Nikki, what brings you over here? Have you decided to build a new development?"

"No more than you've had a sudden urge to buy a house in the suburbs."

He grinned. "You're right, I'll keep my loft instead. When shall I pick you up?" She must have looked a little blank, for he went on, "For dinner tomorrow."

"Oh—that's why I came, actually. It's been put off till another time." Nikki closed the clasps of her briefcase. "I didn't think you'd mind. You were sort of shanghaied into the invitation in the first place—and you must have plenty to do, to get everything finished that Emily Cooper will want done before Sunday."

"Just because she wants every detail finished doesn't mean it'll happen. Hurrying around to complete a job—cutting corners and getting in a rush—is asking for trouble."

So if he hadn't been rushing off to work at Emily Cooper's house, what had been his hurry this morning? *Three guesses, Nikki,* she told herself drearily. *He couldn't wait to get away from you, and the babies, and the whole situation. He was tired of playing with baby dolls. Playing house.*

"That's too bad," he said. "I was looking forward to it."

It was like picking at a scab, but Nikki couldn't stop herself. "To what? The possibility of a job remodeling for them?"

"To the dinner. I liked your friends, Nikki. They seemed like an interesting couple of people."

The blonde had quietly opened the door of Seth's office again, and she was leaning easily against the jamb, her arms folded over her chest, her ankles crossed, in a pose worthy of a magazine cover. "Hi, Seth." Her voice was much lower and more sultry than when she'd been talking to Nora. "Won't you introduce me?"

Seth didn't miss a beat. "Ingrid, this is my friend Nikki."

Friend.

Nikki went through the motions, smiling and shaking hands.

The blonde showed so many pure white teeth that she looked like a shark. She moved away from the door to stand beside Seth. "I'm sure you won't mind if we don't stay and chat," she murmured to Nikki, "but we have a table reserved for lunch." She let her hand slide slowly and intimately down the inside of his sleeve to rest on his elbow.

Reserved where? Nikki wanted to ask. *With some hotel's room service?* "Of course I don't mind," she said. "I'm running late myself—I'm on my way to the bank."

"Tell Richard hello for me," Seth said.

"I'll do that. Thanks, Nora."

Nikki's car was parked closer to the door than Seth's SUV was, and with an almost automatic gesture he opened the driver's door for her as they passed. "Are you okay, Nikki?" he asked, quietly. "You're acting a bit strange."

"Just tired, I guess." She sat behind the wheel, watching from the corner of her eye as he helped the blonde into the SUV.

Acting a bit strange, was she?

Face it head-on, Nikki told herself. *It isn't going to help a bit to dodge the truth.*

Days ago, before she had realized what was really happening to her, she had invited Seth to be her friend—and he was taking her up on it.

It was just her bad luck that suddenly she wanted to be so much more than friends.

Emily Cooper's house had looked like a magazine spread on the night Nikki had first driven Neil Hamilton past—the night he had lost his mind and fallen in love with it. But on the evening of Emily's housewarming party, it looked even better.

There wasn't so much as a leaf out of place, or a blade of grass at the wrong angle. The entire lot glowed; every shrub on the property must have been wired with soft spotlights. Not harsh white ones, either, Nikki noticed. The bulbs had a faint pink cast which made the house look ever so slightly surreal, as if it were floating in a sunset-colored cloud. She made a mental note to remember that trick.

But for now, she knew, she had to focus on Neil Hamilton. As she parked her car around the corner from the big Mediterranean house, she took a long look at Neil, in the passenger seat. "Remember," she prompted. "You're going to a party—that's all. You are not touring a house to decide whether you want to buy it."

He frowned.

Nikki smothered a sigh and tried once again to explain the fine points. "It's perfectly legitimate for me to ask you to escort me to a party," she said. "And if you happen to look around the house and decide you like it, it's perfectly all right for me to call up the owner tomorrow, tell her I'm in real estate, and ask if she'd like to sell it. But it's not all right for me to take you through a house that the owner doesn't want to show. So don't forget—we're only going to a party."

In the hope that you'll hate the house and that will be

the end of it, she added. Of course, telling Neil that would probably only make him want it even more.

"The whole idea tonight is just to see whether you're interested or not," she added. "So don't go prying into closets or checking out the size of medicine cabinets. All that can come later."

He didn't look convinced.

A tap on the car window beside her made Nikki jump, and she turned to see Seth bending down beside the car. She lowered the window.

"Are you coming inside, or chickening out?" he asked.

Nikki looked past him. At least there was no blonde attached to his arm tonight.

Not that it would matter if he had brought someone, she told herself. She would behave just the same, whether he was alone or not.

She'd been through all this while she was getting dressed. No more *acting a bit strange,* as he had put it on Friday. She must—she *would*—get herself back to normal. Back to the way things had been before that week out of time had changed everything for her.

So she smiled at him and said, "I thought you were bringing the X-ray equipment so we could just sit here in the car and look through the walls. But since you seem to have let me down, I guess we'll have to come in." She slid out of the car, not realizing that Seth had stepped aside barely far enough to leave her room to stand. She was practically toe to toe with him. The closeness, and the light scent of his aftershave, made her feel just a little dizzy, and Nikki had to take a grip on herself. "Neil doesn't seem to quite get the ethics of the situation yet," she said softly.

Seth nodded. "I'll try to intercept if he starts to talk to anyone."

And that will keep both of you busy, Nikki thought, so I can relax a bit.

Throngs of people streamed up the sidewalk toward the house. What Emily called a housewarming party looked more like a gathering for a major sporting event, Nikki thought, except that everyone was dressed up. She'd never seen so many precious gems in one place in her life.

Strains of classical music wafted from the open main doorway, where a butler in white tie and tails stood, directing traffic. "The ladies' cloakroom is upstairs to the right," he told Nikki with a tiny bow. "Gentlemen, upstairs and to the left."

Which meant that they could get a pretty good glimpse of the entire upper floor, Nikki thought. How very sweet of Emily to arrange it so easily.

At the top of the stairs, she stood on her toes to whisper into Seth's ear. "I'll meet you right back here in ten minutes. Try to make sure he doesn't go prying behind closed doors, all right?"

She left her velvet jacket on the brass bed in the company of an entire zoo full of furs, combed her hair, reapplied her lipstick, and went back out to the hallway. Seth was lounging at the top of the stairs; Neil was standing where he could get a look now and then into the guest room the ladies were using.

"He looks like a Peeping Tom," she muttered to Seth. "Come on, let's go downstairs. You know, Emily didn't strike me as the type who would hire a string quartet."

"Hire them, yes. Enjoy them, no."

"Well, maybe you're right." Nikki went to retrieve Neil. "Seth and I are going to circulate slowly through the whole house," she said. "If you just follow behind, you can get a good look at everything because we'll be a sort of screen for you. You don't have to talk to anybody, you don't have to think—just look. But stay close, all right?'' She laid a hand on his elbow and urged him downstairs.

Nikki had been in real estate long enough to know lots of people, and Emily Cooper seemed to know them all, too. Before they'd crossed the main hallway to the big living room, Nikki had counted three couples to whom she'd sold houses in the neighborhood. And Seth had his own crowd of clients and acquaintances to greet.

The problem, Nikki soon realized, was not going to be moving slowly enough so Neil could take in all the details of the house. The difficulty would be managing to get through all the rooms before the party was over.

Seth stopped a waiter with a tray full of champagne glasses. Nikki sipped and chatted and tried not to look at the house itself. It was all up to Neil now anyway. Either he'd like it or he wouldn't. If he did, she'd deal with that complication tomorrow, and probably end up knowing a great deal more about the house than she wanted to. If he didn't like it, there was no point in her looking around, drawing attention to herself.

While Seth was talking to a long-time customer, Nikki let her gaze veer across the room, and she spotted Richard watching her from near the blazing fireplace. ''You didn't tell me Richard was going to be here,'' she said under her breath as soon as Seth's customer had moved off.

''I didn't help assemble the guest list, sweetheart. My contribution was limited to suggesting she hire a jazz band instead of the strings.''

Emily Cooper herself, wearing a peach taffeta gown and a sort of turban built of feathers, came up just then and gave Seth a playful swat on the wrist with her folded fan. ''Jazz would have been far too loud,'' she said. She leaned around Seth. ''And—my goodness—who is this?'' She didn't take her eyes off Neil, but she was clearly addressing

Nikki. "Your husband? No, you said you didn't have one right now. So what brings this nice man to my party?"

I'm busted, Nikki thought. Being caught crashing the party was bad enough, but if Neil let slip why she'd brought him along…

Worse, Seth's customer had returned with one last question and drew him a few steps away to talk to someone else. So Seth was going to be no help at all. Nikki was strictly on her own.

"Neil's new to Kansas City," Nikki said quickly. "Seth and I knew he'd meet the nicest people here."

Emily was holding out a hand to Neil. He had dragged his attention from the frieze which decorated the built-in bookcases and turned his attention to his unintentional hostess.

Nikki heard Emily take in a breath, and abruptly she remembered the effect when she'd first met Neil and thought she'd walked into an old-time motion picture. Or did that hiss of Emily's mean that she recognized him from somewhere? Did she know why he was there?

Nikki felt a tap on her shoulder and turned to see Richard. "Oh—hi. Sorry, Richard, but I can't talk right now. Really."

Richard didn't seem to hear her. "I thought you told me there was nobody else."

Nikki was aggravated. Hadn't the man been listening that night outside her front door? "No," she corrected. "To be precise, I told you that it wasn't really any of your business whether there was or wasn't."

"Oh, yes, that's right." Richard's gaze had flicked across the crowd to rest on Seth, now standing several feet away and still talking to the customer. "So that's the guy you've chosen, eh?" He shook his head, but his expression seemed to be confused rather than disapproving. "Odd."

Nikki bit her tongue and told herself not to ask, but she couldn't let the remark pass. "I don't know why you'd assume that, just because we happen to be attending the same party. But even if it were true, what would be so odd about it?"

"That you'd go for him." Richard looked directly at her. "The guy who broke up your last engagement."

She couldn't believe she'd heard him correctly. "Seth didn't break up anything. You're misinformed."

"He was there, wasn't he?"

She was suddenly back in the church, on the day that was supposed to have been her wedding day, facing her fiancé—and seeing Seth behind the pillar. "He saw the fight, if that's what you mean. But he didn't cause it."

"Sure of that, are you? And you don't know why he was there?"

Nikki was beginning to feel impatient. "He was there because he was his brother's best man. Stephen was getting married that day too, so of course Seth was at the church. Richard, you aren't even making sense!"

"He made sure he was there to see the effects of his little prank."

"Prank?"

"Yeah. Hiring the call girls for your fiancé's bachelor party. Excuse me, exotic dancers."

"Richard, he wasn't even at Thorpe's bachelor party."

"I didn't say he went. I said he sent the girls. Didn't you ever wonder why they showed up?"

Not exactly, Nikki thought. Thorpe had always sworn he'd had no idea where the dancers had come from, or why they'd appeared at his bachelor party. Nikki had assumed that his pals had taken up a collection to pay the bill—with the groom's tacit permission.

But to associate Seth with the whole affair was out-landish.

"So you didn't know that, did you?" Richard said shrewdly. "But then I'm sure he wasn't eager to tell you about it, considering what happened."

"Or anyone else, I imagine," Nikki said dryly. "So how do you know all this?"

"Steve told me. He thought it was a great practical joke. A harmless, funny little prank—until it ended by breaking up your wedding." Richard sipped his champagne and added meditatively, "So I guess it's no wonder Seth never bothered to tell you what *really* happened."

CHAPTER TEN

HE WAS mistaken, Nikki told herself. That was the only possible answer. Richard certainly had not witnessed the confrontation, or heard Thorpe's feeble explanations. But Nikki had been there, and she knew exactly what had—and hadn't—happened.

Yet Richard seemed so sure of himself that she almost doubted her own perceptions. Was it logical to think that this entire tale could have risen out of nothing more than his own jealous feelings? He surely must have had some cause.

Steve told me…

That much was possible, Nikki admitted, because Richard did indeed know Stephen. Nikki had introduced the two of them herself not long after the double-wedding-that-wasn't, when Stephen and Laura had first started looking for financing to buy a house.

…He thought it was a great practical joke.

And she had to concede that was possible, too. Stephen was reliable and steady now, but there was no question that he'd sowed a few wild oats before he'd settled down with Laura. There had been a point in his life when he might well have thought that sending a gift package of exotic dancers to a bachelor party was a hilarious trick. Nikki didn't get the humor, but perhaps it was one of those guy things that no woman could ever fully understand.

But to tell another man about it…how well did Stephen know Richard, anyway? Well enough to share that kind of back-slapping tale about his brother? Surely not. Unless perhaps Stephen himself had been involved, and he was bragging about his own idea rather than Seth's. Maybe Stephen had only dragged Seth into it to keep Laura from finding out....

This, she thought, was all getting much too complicated.

The room felt hot, crowded, noisy. Nikki looked around, hoping to see a path to an open window or a door where she could get a breath of fresh air, and abruptly realized that while she'd been absorbed in Richard's story, Neil had vanished. She wondered for an instant if Emily had discovered why he was there and thrown him out. Unlikely, she decided, because if she had suspected, Nikki herself would have probably gotten the boot right along with him.

That should have been a relief, but it left her wondering where he'd gone instead. There were sixteen rooms in Emily Cooper's house, counting those in the new wing, and Nikki had no idea which direction he'd gone or where to start looking.

Seth reappeared beside her. "Sorry that discussion took so long. They like Emily's new wing so well they're thinking of building one themselves. Where's Neil?"

"I lost him," she admitted. "Or else he heard the Pied Piper go by and joined the parade."

"Along with the rest of the rats? How unflattering of you. How did you manage to lose him, anyway? He was right behind us."

"I got so incredibly involved in this story Richard was telling me that I forgot to keep an eye on Neil."

"If it was good enough to take your mind off your client, you'll have to share it sometime."

"If I can remember all the details." She faced Seth squarely. "But perhaps you've already heard it. It was about a bachelor party and a bunch of exotic dancers."

"I hope it had a good punch line." He sounded almost

absentminded, and he was looking around as if searching for Neil.

"I was more interested in the cast," Nikki said. "You see, Richard told me you and Stephen are the ones who sent the dancers to Thorpe's bachelor party."

"I wonder what would make him say that."

So it wasn't true after all. But not until relief oozed through Nikki's muscles did she realize how tense the whole thing had made her. How foolish it was of her to get so upset over something Richard had told her, something that he'd so obviously misunderstood. After the way he'd assumed that a few dates gave him the right to know where she was all the time, she should have known better than to credit anything he said.

And yet...there had been something in Seth's voice which set off warning chimes in her head. Surely he should have been shocked by the accusation, not just mildly surprised...

"Because," Seth said levelly, "Steve didn't have anything to do with it."

The words struck her with the force of an explosion. Nikki could feel the parquet floor rocking under her feet. "Which means you did?"

He looked her straight in the eye. "Yes. I did."

Richard had been right, then. Absolutely right—for he had not accused Stephen at all, only Seth. That extra part of the story had come from her own analysis, her own reasoning. *Your own attempt to dilute the responsibility and make excuses for Seth. If his brother was in on it, too, then he didn't seem as guilty.*

She took a breath, preparing to slice him with the edge of her tongue, but instead she heard herself asking what must be the stupidest question of all time. "Why didn't you ever tell me?"

Seth's voice was very low. "You never asked me till now."

"Oh, sure—like I went around quizzing everyone I knew about who'd done it!"

"Nikki, come on. I did you a favor."

She pounced. "Then why weren't you eager to stand up and take credit for it? Don't be a hypocrite, Seth."

"Would you have gone ahead and married him if you'd known he hadn't hired the call girls himself?"

"I *never* thought he hired them."

"Then what difference does it make who paid the bill?"

Nikki bit her lip, trying to get it clear in her own mind. However the dancers had gotten to the party, the fact was that Thorpe had thoroughly enjoyed them. That was the reason she'd called off the wedding. But that fact didn't make Seth's action snow-white and squeaky clean. "Because it was a dirty trick, Seth."

"No, it wasn't. I provided the temptation, yes. But he's the one who decided to surrender to it."

"Obviously we'll have to agree to disagree on that one. Why did you do it, anyway? You weren't even there to watch the fun."

"You think I'd want to watch him make a fool of himself?"

"Then why bother? Because you were curious? Because it gave you some kind of cheap thrill?"

"Well, I wouldn't exactly call it cheap." He obviously saw her eyes narrow, for he added hastily, "I'm sorry, Nikki. I shouldn't have said that."

"You know precisely what I mean. Having power—playing with people's lives…"

"I didn't make him do anything. I don't know why you're getting so bent out of shape about something that's—"

"Do not *dare* to tell me this is none of my business."

"I was going to say, something that's over and done with. You told me yourself you'd put it all behind you and you didn't want to talk about Thorpe—or even think about him—any more."

"That was when I thought it was only me we were talking about. Before I knew you were involved." She squeezed her eyes shut, trying to stop the hot prickle of tears. "It was just a joke to you, wasn't it? Like a beer-chugging contest. 'Let's see if we can make Thorpe act like a jackass.' Did you place bets on it? Start a pool about how long he'd hold out?"

"Nikki, come on. You're upset—" He reached out for her arm.

"You'd better believe I am." She pulled away from him. "When you see Neil again, tell him to take a cab back to the hotel and send me the bill."

She'd never before realized how much of an advantage it was to be small-boned and tiny, but she could slide through gaps in the crowd that Seth—or for that matter, even those tall blondes he favored—could never fit through. She was out the front door before he was able to cross the room. She'd left her jacket behind in Emily Cooper's guest room, and her car felt frigid—or was that just the aftereffect of the shock she'd had? She was trembling so hard it was difficult even to start the car. But she had to get away from Rockhurst.

It would be awful if Seth came after her and found her crying. And it would be even worse if he didn't bother to follow her at all.

She drove past the art museum, closed but lit with a wash of spotlights over the huge Corinthian columns, past Union Station with its bright banners, past the stark column of the Liberty Memorial. Finally she parked her car on the plaza beyond the memorial, where she could look at the lights of the city, each turned into a starburst by the tears in her eyes.

So this was the answer. After two years, endless self-questioning, and hundreds of crumpled tissues, she finally knew exactly why she and Thorpe hadn't made it to the altar.

But deep down, it wasn't regret over her failed engagement that was gnawing at her. No matter what the source of his excuse had been, Thorpe had shown his true colors at that bachelor party. She'd made the right decision—the only one she could have lived with. Better a short-term embarrassment than a long-term disaster.

What was bothering Nikki was the reason Seth had done it. It hadn't been because he cared about her, but because he'd been mildly curious about what would happen if he pulled a few strings.

She had fallen in love with a man who'd looked at her as if she were some sort of laboratory animal. Someone who thought her life was merely an interesting kind of experiment.

It took effort, but Nikki kept a smile on her face as she helped Laura with the final preparations for the twins' birthday party. There were two cakes to set out, two piles of packages to arrange, two bunches of party hats to assemble, and a limited time to do it all before the babies woke from their nap and the guests started to arrive.

She was standing on a stepladder hanging crepe paper streamers over the dining room table when Laura said casually, "Did Seth tell you he's going to bring over a helium tank to do the balloons?"

It was almost a relief to have it out in the open, because Nikki had been waiting for the mention of his name ever since she'd arrived. Frankly she was surprised that Laura had held out for the better part of two hours before indulging her curiosity.

Not that Nikki was going to rise to so feeble a bait. "He didn't mention it. But then I haven't seen him for a couple of weeks."

She also didn't intend to volunteer that on the last occasion she had seen Seth, he had *not* seen her. When he'd come by the real-estate office to drop off the jacket she'd left at Emily's party, she'd been standing beside Jen's desk and spotted the SUV in the parking lot. So she'd pleaded with Jen to cover for her, and Nikki had run for the washroom...

"He hasn't been hanging around here much," Laura said. "And when you said you weren't bringing Richard to the party, I thought maybe..."

"You mean you added two and two and got sixteen. Right?"

Laura shot a sideways look at Nikki. "You can't blame me for hoping."

Nikki told herself to keep everything casual, to appear relaxed, to react just as she would have a few weeks ago— back when she and Seth were still just acquaintances. If she could only remember how things had been, back then...

Just acquaintances. But that wasn't quite true, she realized. Even in the early days, when she hadn't been paying conscious attention to Seth Baxter, he'd still drawn her like a magnet. Why should she have cared how he looked at her? Why should she even have noticed the expression on his face whenever he spotted her?

Because you were already painfully aware of him, she admitted. *Because you already wanted him to look at you very differently. Without wariness, without bemusement— and with love.*

She kept her voice light, but it took effort. "Cut it out, Laura, or I'll tell Seth you're a Machiavellian match-maker—that you arranged for that virus to hit the cruise ship, and that you broke the dishwasher on purpose so he'd have to come over here and spend time with me."

"If I'd thought it would work," Laura said comfortably, "I might have done exactly that. You'd make a good combination, you know."

I thought so too—for a while. Nikki climbed down off the stepladder and inspected her work. "I think that'll do. If we're finished with the ladder, I'll take it back to the garage."

"Yes—and would you bring in the ice cream from the freezer? I told Stephen to leave it out there."

Nikki was halfway out the door when she saw that Seth's SUV was in the driveway. He must have arrived while she was decorating. The garage door was open, and he and Stephen were inside, filling balloons from a tall tank of helium. Apparently he'd been there for a while because the bunch of balloons was already huge.

And he'd obviously seen her. It was too late to retreat, for it would create far too much interest if she tried to dodge him. So she pasted a smile on her face and went on to the garage.

Seth tied a knot in the neck of a balloon and reached for the stepladder, easily hanging it back on the ceiling hook reserved for it. Nikki thanked him and went on to the freezer, tucked into the back of the garage. She dug around for a while and then turned to the men. "Laura said the ice cream was in the freezer. But where?"

"Ice cream?" Stephen said. "Damn, I forgot to pick up the ice cream. Seth, move your SUV so I can get my car out."

Seth dug into his pocket and tossed him a set of keys instead. "We'll cover for you."

"We?" Nikki said as the SUV zoomed out of the drive-way.

"Yeah. If you go back in without the ice cream, Laura will know he forgot it."

"And you think she won't figure that out anyway?"

"Besides, ice cream reminds me—I picked up the proofs of the kids' pictures." He pointed at a lightweight jacket tossed across the hood of Laura's car. "Take a look if you like."

Keep it light. Keep it casual. Nikki picked up the jacket and took a package out of the pocket. The flannel lining still felt warm from his body heat, and she wanted to snuggle it close in her arms. Instead, she laid the jacket back on the car and opened the envelope.

Everything seemed brighter in the pictures than it was in her memory. She didn't remember the ice cream being quite so pink, or the twins' faces quite so intent, or the mess they had made before it was all over being quite such a disaster. And she certainly didn't remember looking at Seth with quite that adoring expression in her eyes—but one of the shots had caught the two of them standing on each side of the stroller, and the look on her face was em-barrassingly intimate.

It was all the evidence necessary to prove that even then, long before she'd realized it, she'd been falling in love.

She shot a glance at Seth, who seemed absorbed in the helium tank, and slid that proof into the pocket of her jeans.

Even if he'd already seen the picture, she told herself, he might not have recognized the expression on her face because he wouldn't have been expecting it. But, if he took the pictures inside to share at the party, Laura wouldn't miss it. And if anyone commented, and raised Seth's suspicions…

No, Nikki decided. She would just hang onto that particular proof until she could return it herself.

And as long as she was going to stop at the photographer's studio anyway…

She sneaked another look at Seth and then nicked a second picture from the package and added it to her pocket. It was not, perhaps, the best photograph ever taken of Seth, since he was only in the background and the twins were the stars. But he was smiling…his eyes were gleaming…he looked at ease and contented.

"Not bad," she said. She put the package back with his jacket, picked up a handful of limp balloons, and passed a red one to him. "I didn't buy leashes for the kids' gift after all."

"Then it's a good thing I didn't waste time looking at rhinestone dog collars."

"Actually, Anna would probably have liked one. The more garish, the better. She's getting seriously into sparkly things."

Seth shuddered. "I thought girls waited till they were at least five to do that."

"I'm afraid they're born with it. How is Emily Cooper's addition going?"

"It's all finished. We turned over the key last Friday." He looked at her almost curiously. "You haven't talked to her lately, have you?"

"No. Neil hasn't called me since the housewarming party, so I thought there was no point in pursuing Emily to ask if she wanted to sell." Nikki forced her voice to stay steady. "After the way I dumped him, I can't say I'm surprised not to hear from him. But I must admit I wonder if that means he doesn't want the house anymore, or if he's just found another real-estate person to act for him.''

"He doesn't know you dumped him."

Nikki frowned.

"I didn't give him your message that night," Seth said. "I took him back to the hotel instead. I figured it was the least I could do."

Nikki thought he was right on target there, since he was the one who had caused all the trouble. She supposed it should be comforting to know that he'd learned something from the whole debacle.

"Of course," Seth added meditatively, "he didn't stay there."

"Who? Neil? Where did he go?"

"Back to Emily's. I'm not sure when he actually moved—but he's living there now."

Nikki's jaw dropped. "I had no idea he wanted the house *that* badly." She clapped a hand over her mouth. "I mean…"

"That Emily would be no prize to live with? Neither is Neil, of course, but they seem to be quite smitten with each other. As long as we're talking about what happened at the party, Nikki—"

"Which party are you referring to?"

He didn't seem to hear the ice in her voice. "You asked me why I did it—why I sent the dancers to Thorpe's bachelor party. But then you didn't want to listen to the answer."

"I didn't have to hear it. You did it because you were curious. You just wanted to see what would happen if you prodded him."

"Like poking a rattlesnake with a stick? That's true, up to a point. But it's not the whole story."

"I don't see why you should want to tell me all about

it now, when you didn't say a word about it for two years, Seth."

"I did it," he said meditatively, "because I didn't think he was good enough for you. And I wondered whether he'd prove it, if he was offered enough temptation."

Nikki thought it over while he blew up four more balloons. It took that long for her to get herself under control enough to trust her voice. "You thought he wasn't good enough for me?"

"That's what I said, yes."

Maybe I wasn't just an experiment. Maybe he really did care—at least a little.

"And what made that any of your business, Seth? You're surely not going to expect me to believe that you were interfering because you were nursing some wild secret infatuation for me." She was proud of herself—she thought her voice held just the right tone of cynical sarcasm, just the right shade of disbelief. Even a faint tinge of horror at the very idea. "Because you wanted me for yourself?"

"No. No, I didn't have a wild secret infatuation for you." He sounded very calm. Apparently the accusation wasn't important enough—or ridiculous enough—to get upset about.

Nikki's chest constricted until she could barely breathe. What a fool she was. Even as she had told herself that he didn't care, she had still allowed herself to hope that down deep he must have felt the tiniest spark of what she had found in her heart for him.

This must be why people spoke of their hopes being crushed—because that was exactly what it felt like when the last feeble flicker was smashed out of existence.

She said quietly, "You were right, Seth. You did me a favor. It was Thorpe's nature to cheat. If he hadn't had the opportunity at the bachelor party, he'd have found it at the country club, or at work, or in a friend's house.'' She swallowed hard. ''Thank you. End of subject—all right?''

''No, it's not all right. You asked me why I did it. That was my reason—back then.''

She closed her eyes in pain. ''You know, it really isn't necessary to do a full autopsy on this decision, Seth.''

''I wasn't even attracted to you. I was just interested.''

Nikki's voice was taut. ''Spare me the definitions, all right?''

''But when you started dating again within a week of breaking your engagement, I was more than interested, I was fascinated. Every time I saw you, you were with a different guy.''

''I was playing the field,'' Nikki said crisply.

Seth shook his head. ''No, you weren't. Playing the field means dating lots of people. But each time I ran across you, you were seeing only one guy—exclusively, and apparently very seriously. Then the next time, there would be a different guy. It was like you were trying to work your way through the entire Kansas City phone book, one man at a time. For a while, I couldn't figure out what you were doing.''

''I'm sure you're going to tell me what you decided, whether I want to hear it or not.''

''You were serious about the man of the moment right up to the point where he got serious about you—and then you dropped him. You were making sure no one could hurt you again the way Thorpe had.''

He was only partly correct, Nikki thought. He was right that she'd dated only one guy at a time, but she hadn't been serious about any one of them. However, Seth's perception of what she was doing explained the way he had habitually surveyed her with mingled fascination and irony, and then turned his attention away as if he couldn't bear to look any

longer. Not that it was a lot of comfort to understand what
he'd been thinking. "You might as well call me a man-
eating shark and be done with it," she said.

"I thought that's what you were. But that week we spent
with the babies—as I got to know you…the picture didn't
fit with the label any more."

"Well, that's comforting," she said dryly.

"It was only then I admitted what was happening to
me." He filled the last balloon, tied it into the bunch, and
leaned against the fender of Laura's car. "Though I think
it must have actually started happening way back when I
met you and Thorpe and decided you didn't fit together."

Nikki's hands started to tremble. *Don't do this to yourself,* she ordered. *You've gotten your hopes up before, only
to have them smashed.*

"I've thought about it a lot, the last couple of weeks,"
Seth said quietly. "About whether I should just leave things
alone and go back to the way it was. But I don't think I
can. That night when I came into the house and you'd fixed
dinner—you were lighting candles on the dining room table, and the candlelight glowed on your hair in such a
strange way… For just an instant, it looked like you were
wearing a wedding veil."

Nikki tried to hold back the tears. She'd been afraid of
something like that. He'd looked at her so oddly that
night… And now she knew that no matter how innocent
she'd told herself that dinner was, she had been trying to
show him what he was missing. She had already wanted
more than just friendship. No wonder he'd suspected her
of being manipulative. He'd understood what she was up
to even better than Nikki herself had.

Seth mused, "And I realized that's why I'd been so certain from the beginning that you and Thorpe didn't fit to-

gether. It was because all along I wanted you to fit with me.''

Her throat was so tight she couldn't speak, couldn't even make a noise.

''I was starting to think that maybe you felt the same way. That it wasn't just a matter of getting along for the sake of the babies... Until that day on the Plaza when we were in the carriage and you saw Richard and ducked down behind Zack. You didn't want him to see you with me, did you?''

''No,'' she said. It was barely a croak. ''I didn't.''

Seth sighed. ''I shouldn't have said anything at all, I suppose, because we can't exactly avoid these family occasions.''

Family occasions, she thought wistfully. *If only I was really a part of the family...*

''I thought it would be better to bring it out in the open,'' he said. ''But now I've just made things uncomfortable, haven't I—because I can't miss things like the twins' birthdays, and I'm not asking you to stay away either. I'm sorry. I'd just hoped... There's one more thing I have to know, Nikki, and then I'll shut up. Which picture did you take out of the package just now?''

The question was so unexpected that before she'd realized it, Nikki had tripped herself up. ''How did you know I— You weren't even looking this direction!''

''I don't have to look,'' he said quietly. ''When you're anywhere around, I know what you're doing.''

She was shaking so much now that she couldn't get hold of the proofs in her pocket. Finally she gave up and braced her hands against the car to lessen the trembling. ''I didn't want Richard to see us together that day,'' she said. ''But not because I was ashamed of being with you, Seth. It was because I didn't want him to spoil the magic by getting possessive and asking questions.''

''He was getting serious about you.''

She nodded. ''Yes. But you're wrong about my reasons, Seth. I wasn't trying to get even with Thorpe. I wasn't serious about any of those guys. I just made it look that way when you were around, because…because I didn't want you to think I was at loose ends. You were always with one of your ghastly blondes—and I didn't want you to know…'' She swallowed hard. *Now or never,* she told herself, and looked straight at him. ''I didn't want you to know that even then, I was waiting for you. Because if you'd known I was free—and you didn't care…''

Before she could finish the sentence, he'd pulled her away from the car, and she was in his arms.

''It was easier just to pretend that the blondes didn't matter,'' she whispered.

''But they didn't matter, honey. They were a distraction, that's all.'' He seemed to decide that action was better than explanation, and his mouth came down on hers—hard, possessive, sure of himself, and yet with a gentle understanding that rocked her more than pure passion could ever have done.

Even when he stopped kissing her, he didn't relax his hold, and Nikki was glad of it, for she suspected she couldn't have stood up on her own. Something seemed to be seriously wrong with her knees. ''What about Ingrid?''

''Ingrid?'' His voice had a sandpapery edge to it. ''You mean Ingrid Anderson? Did she bother you?''

''Of course not,'' Nikki said tartly.

Seth grinned. ''Right. She bothered me, too. We were supposed to have a business lunch with her husband that day to discuss my bid to build their new house, but after that performance in my office I decided not to go after the job. Of course, after Zack chewed up their floor plans, I might not have gotten it anyway.''

Nikki's jaw dropped. ''But you acted as if—''

''Well, of course I did,'' Seth said. ''If a gorgeous woman flings herself at me in front of one I'm trying to make jealous, I'm going to play it for all it's—''

She drew back and made a face at him.

Seth laughed and tugged her closer. ''Show me the pictures in your pocket,'' he whispered.

She pulled the two snapshots out. Seth took them, keeping one arm around her as he held the pictures at arm's length. ''Interesting choice. I particularly like the one of you—I ordered an enlargement of that one already. But I think we can do better.''

''Oh?''

''Yes. White gown, tuxedo, flowers instead of ice-cream cones… Marry me, Nikki?''

''I'll have to think about it,'' Nikki said simply. ''For one thing, twins seem to run in your family, and I don't know if I could—''

''We did pretty well with these two. Think what we could accomplish with regular practice.''

''That's true.'' She took a deep breath. ''All right. I'll take a chance on you.''

''Good. Let's go announce it. Zack and Anna won't care if we trump their birthday party, as long as we promise they can smear cake all over our wedding, too.''

But Nikki didn't move. She smiled and tugged his mouth down to hers once more, luxuriating in the freedom to hold him, to kiss him.

''Well, I guess there's no real hurry about spreading the news,'' Seth said huskily.

It was the purr of an approaching engine which drew them back to the present. The SUV pulled into the driveway, and Stephen got out, cradling two half-gallons of ice cream in one arm, his other hand at his brow, shading his eyes as he stared into the shadow of the garage. He looked stunned.

The back door banged and Laura came out. "Stephen! You'll never guess what just happened!"

"Now wait a minute," Seth groaned. "How on earth could she possibly know...?"

"A courier just made a special delivery," Laura gasped. "Because of the mess-up on our cruise, they've given us another one to make up for it. Can you believe it? Seth? Nikki? Any chance you two would agree to baby-sit again? Stephen, what on earth are you goggling at?"

Stephen didn't answer. He just pointed at the garage, where Seth and Nikki were still standing in each other's arms.

Laura turned toward the garage, took a long look, and smiled. "Well, it's about time you two came to your senses."

Seth moved a little. "Thank you," he said. "And as for your question, Laura, the answer is no. At least not until we've had a cruise of our own. Talk to us again after the honeymoon."

And he drew Nikki close once more, shutting out the world.

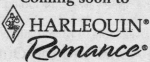
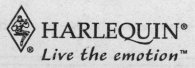

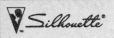

The world's bestselling romance series.

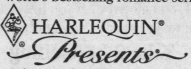

HARLEQUIN®
Presents
Seduction and Passion Guaranteed!

Legally wed, but he's never said…
"I love you."

They're…

Wedlocked!

The series
where
marriages are
made in haste…
and love
comes later…

**Look out for more Wedlocked! marriage stories in
Harlequin Presents throughout 2005**

Coming in March:
HIS BRIDE FOR ONE NIGHT by Miranda Lee, #2451

Coming in April:
THE BILLION-DOLLAR BRIDE by Kay Thorpe, #2462

Coming in May:
THE DISOBEDIENT BRIDE by Helen Bianchin, #2463

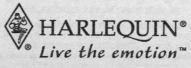

HARLEQUIN®
Live the emotion™

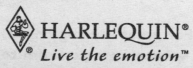